To Sara 🩷

All The Teacher's Beasts

N.J.

N.J. ADEL

Adel

ALL THE TEACHER'S BEASTS

THIS IS A WORK OF FICTION. ALL INCIDENTS AND DIALOGUE, AND ALL CHARACTERS ARE PRODUCTS OF THE AUTHOR'S IMAGINATION. ANY RESEMBLANCE TO PERSONS LIVING OR DEAD IS ENTIRELY COINCIDENTAL.

ALL CHARACTERS DEPICTED ARE OVER THE AGE OF 18.

NO PART OF THIS PUBLICATION MAY BE REPRODUCED, DISTRIBUTED OR TRANSMITTED IN ANY FORM OR BY ANY MEANS, INCLUDING PHOTOCOPYING, RECORDING, OR OTHER ELECTRONIC OR MECHANICAL METHODS, WITHOUT THE PRIOR WRITTEN PERMISSION OF THE AUTHOR, EXCEPT IN THE CASE OF BRIEF QUOTATIONS EMBODIED IN CRITICAL REVIEWS AND CERTAIN OTHER NONCOMMERCIAL USES PERMITTED BY COPYRIGHT LAW. FOR PERMISSION REQUESTS, WRITE TO THE AUTHOR AT THE E-MAIL ADDRESS BELOW.

N.J.ADEL.MAJESTY@GMAIL.COM

Copyright © 2019 N.J. Adel
All rights reserved.
ISBN: 9781705782903
Salacious Queen Publishing

DEDICATION

To all the loving beasts
To vampires, werewolves and devils
To villains we now understand and crave

CONTENTS

DEDICATION III
CONTENTS V
Also by N.J. Adel IX
BEFORE YOU READ X
CHAPTER 1 1
    BELLE 1
CHAPTER 2 13
    BELLE 13
CHAPTER 3 19
    BELLE 19
CHAPTER 4 37
    BELLE 37
CHAPTER 5 41
    ALEC 41
CHAPTER 6 46
    BELLE 46
CHAPTER 7 52
    BELLE 52
CHAPTER 8 62

JOSHUA 62
CHAPTER 9 69
  BELLE 69
CHAPTER 10 75
  BELLE 75
CHAPTER 11 85
  ALEC 85
CHAPTER 12 90
  KAYDEN 90
CHAPTER 13 103
  BELLE 103
CHAPTER 14 112
  JOSHUA 112
CHAPTER 15 115
  BELLE 115
CHAPTER 16 119
  BELLE 119
CHAPTER 17 128
  JOSHUA 128
CHAPTER 18 138
  ALEC 138
CHAPTER 19 145
  ALEC 145

CHAPTER 20	157
BELLE	157
CHAPTER 21	165
BELLE	165
CHAPTER 22	176
BELLE	176
CHAPTER 23	180
KAYDEN	180
CHAPTER 24	183
KAYDEN	183
CHAPTER 25	192
BELLE	192
CHAPTER 26	206
BELLE	206
CHAPTER 27	215
BELLE	215
CHAPTER 28	224
BELLE	224
CHAPTER 29	229
JOSHUA	229
CHAPTER 30	237
KAYDEN	237
CHAPTER 31	241

JOSHUA 241
CHAPTER 32 250
BELLE 250
CHAPTER 33 267
BELLE 267
CHAPTER 34 270
BELLE 270
CHAPTER 35 278
BELLE 278
CHAPTER 36 289
BELLE 289
CHAPTER 37 294
KAYDEN 294
CHAPTER 38 299
BELLE 299
CHAPTER 39 306
BELLE 306
CHAPTER 40 321
BELLE 321
Also by N.J. Adel 330
Acknowledgments 331
ABOUT THE AUTHOR 332

ALL THE TEACHER'S BEASTS

Also by N.J. Adel

Reverse Harem Standalones
All the Teacher's Pet Beasts
All the Teacher's Little Belles
All the Teacher's Bad Boys

Reverse Harem Erotic Romance
Her Royal Harem: Complete Box Set

Contemporary Romance
The Italian Heartthrob
The Italian Marriage
The Italian Obsession

Dark MC and Mafia Romance
I Hate You then I Love You Collection
Darkness Between Us
Nine Minutes Later
Nine Minutes Xtra
Nine Minutes Forever

BEFORE YOU READ

Do NOT do the helicopter…

CHAPTER 1
BELLE

"You're wearing the red dress or I'm cutting you," Katrina called from the kitchen.

I tugged on the hem of the miniature dress she gave me, blowing out a breath, and stared at the ridiculous amount of pale leg I was offering up. I hated that my first wonder was if Declan would allow me to wear something that revealing.

Glaring at myself, I shoved the image of the monster's face aside. You'd think this shit we blandly call domestic abuse didn't happen to someone like me, a nerd who was smart enough to get her PhD when she was twenty-five, a Psychology professor herself a year later?

Well, it did.

For years.

Why had I let it go on this long?

The devil I knew… Or so I'd told myself.

Katrina's heels echoed from the kitchen and to my bedroom in eight steps. Yeah, I counted when I was unpacking.

I'd gone from a huge house in California to a tiny Forest Grove apartment slightly bigger than my former living room. The apartment felt even smaller once I'd unpacked, and Katrina asked me at least five times since she'd set foot in it why I'd chosen such a place.

I chose it because it was the only one available when I moved to Oregon in such a hurry without a chance to secure a place to live first.

But I didn't care.

It was unlike anything I'd known since I got married. Plus, the place had giant bay windows framing every room and a forest view. It was beautiful, and I'd never felt happier in the past ten years of my life.

"Give me one good reason why you shouldn't wear this," she said, leaning against the doorframe, her arms crossed over her chest, her boobs perking up even more in that perfect green dress.

"Because you," I gestured at her reflection in the mirror, "are wearing that. I mean, look at your boobs. Your legs are perfectly tanned, but mine... You can pull something like this, but I..." I chuckled and moved away from the mirror, plopping down on the edge of the bed, hoping she'd buy my lie.

She sighed as she sat next to me. "So it has nothing to do with that dick asshole fucker who put you in hospital between life and death—"

"Katrina, please," I interrupted her, barely meeting her huge, green eyes that looked even *greener* with the dress on.

She cocked a brow, staring me down. "Please what?"

I didn't want any recollection of that image today. It was my first birthday without Declan after ten miserable ones, and she drove all the way from Washington to help me celebrate, not to revive one of the worst experiences of my life.

But I didn't want to be a dick to her either. She was my only friend left, the only one who stuck around when everybody else thought *I* was the one driving them away. And I was very thankful she got me this gig here in Oregon. I wouldn't have dreamt of teaching again after…

A troubled sigh escaped my chest. "You must understand he's all I've known for ten years. He's messed up with my head. It's going to take a while before I'm…finally liberated."

Her face softened, and she gave me a hug. "I know, sweetie, and I'm sorry you had to go through this. You're safe now. He can't hurt you anymore." She pulled away and smiled at me. "You can start living the life you deserve. And when is a better time to start than your birthday?"

"Can't think of one."

Her smile turned into a laugh. "That's my girl." She shot up and dashed to the window. "We're drinking and dancing and showing skin."

"I still don't know how much skin I want to show. I'd like to…you know…stay single for a while."

"Not on your birthday. Ever heard of hot, meaningless sex? One night stands?"

My jaw hung low. "Yeah, I…don't do those."

"Tonight, you will. The women at the club will be flaunting their asses, so showing some legs and boobs is mandatory. Besides," she said, pointing to the street below, "it's too late to change. The limo's here."

Swearing in my head, I got into my favorite red pumps I was only allowed to wear at home, for Declan. They made me look as if I was showing more leg, and I barely recognized myself. I looked like a woman who owned her shit. Daring, confident and hot.

At least, that was what the outfit said.

Katrina practically dragged me out to the limo, and we cracked some champagne on the way to the club in Portland—Forest Grove didn't have nightclubs, only bars.

The DJ spun music from a small stage, and flyers plastered all across the front promised she was the *riotest* DJ in town. Whatever that meant. Was that what young, cool people called good things now? I'd been out of that loop for a while.

Neon lights danced in the dark with the writhing bodies packed everywhere. Still, it was nothing like the clubs in California—not that I'd been to many. Declan kept me in the house like a pet. We rarely went anywhere, not even to the beach. We'd been living in one of the sunniest states in the US, and I was as pale as a vampire.

I'd wasted the majority of my twenties on a man I'd thought was my charming mentor. He turned out to be the psycho monster that almost ended my life.

Never again.

I still had two good years in my twenties, and I was not planning on wasting a second of them.

The music vibrated in my bones as we sat at our booth. It had a good view of both the bar and the now-purple dance floor.

"I'll go get us some drinks then we're dancing till we drop." Katrina, already swaying with the beat, left the booth. That woman was full of energy. She was ten years older than I, with two sons, and she looked even younger than I was.

It was all in the soul. Mine was tainted. Scarred. Most of the time, I felt as if it showed on my face, and everybody could see.

But nobody did. Declan was a master in his performance. He made them all believe we were happy. Perfect. I was envied for being the successful, handsome professor's wife. Not just that. I was hated for it. Even by the faculty members who believed I only got my degree and position because of Declan.

Almost breaking a nail, I sighed and ran a

hand through my hair. I should cut that. The asshole loved long black hair and forbade me to cut it. The one time I rebelled and got myself some nice bangs, he slapped me so hard I lost the hearing in my left ear for weeks. Never regained full ability since.

I'm definitely getting a haircut.

I eyed all the beautiful girls on the dance floor, studying their hairstyles. The short ones stood out, especially on girls with long necks. I had a long neck. It would be nice to be able to show that.

According to *The Devil's Advocate* anyway. That was what John Milton told Mary Ann before he seduced her. Damn, Charlize Theron rocked that hairdo, even if she killed herself at the end of the movie.

At least, she died pretty. I was dying with tangled clumps on my head.

My stare wandered around the flipping and swinging until it hit a wall. A very attractive wall, in a dress shirt that defined a ridiculous amount of muscles in one wall…I meant man, holding a drink.

His bright gaze fixed me in place as he lifted his glass to me. He didn't walk; He glided among the bodies, approaching my booth, his eyes reflecting the current colors of the neon strobe lights.

Green. Blue. Purple. Red.

As he got closer, I realized he was even taller and broader than I thought. Huge was the best word to describe his figure.

Would I say the same about his cock?

My eyes bulged at the thought. What the hell had gotten into me?

Quickly, I looked away, my back to the dance floor, and glared at the actual wall in front of me. *Please go away. Please go away!*

If he speaks to me, I'll choke. Or make a completely inappropriate comment about his penis I have yet to see because for some devilish reason that's all I can think about right now.

"Hi, I'm Alec."

Of course, he didn't go away. Of course, he had a sexy name to go with the body. Of course, it would be my luck to meet a man that looked like that just days after swearing off men forever.

My fists clenched, and my eyes squeezed shut for a moment or ten before I twisted in my seat to meet my stranger again. My hair flipped dramatically with the twist as if I was in a shampoo commercial.

I took a breath and held it, now that my eyes were level with his pants, and I could see the outline of his cock even in this light.

Oh my.

He chuckled. "I'm up here."

My cheeks burned. No. Scratch that. My whole body did. I bet I looked redder than my own dress. Did he notice where I was staring? My lungs felt as if they would burst. Yeah, choking seemed to be a good option now.

I looked up—and up. "Where the hell is Katrina?"

His heavy black brows furrowed, but his lips—God, what in the name of spicy yum were these made of?—twitched on a laugh. "I'm guessing Katrina is your wingman?"

Shit, piss and fuck. Did I say that question out loud? Why would he know where she was or who she was? He must be thinking I was a nutcase already.

Why did I care?

"She's my only friend." The words fell out of my mouth, my brain nonexistent. Something was seriously wrong with me in the presence of this…Alec. "I mean the only friend here with me tonight. We're celebrating my birthday, not…picking up guys."

Too much information, Belle. First I tell a total stranger I'm a pathetic woman with one friend, and now he knows when my birthday is. Way to enable stalkers, Professor. Well done.

He helped himself to a seat in my booth, sliding on the leather couch across from me.

"Does that mean it's unlikely you'd leave here with me?"

I couldn't believe this douche right now. "I… What? No."

"That's a pity."

"We just met."

"Yet I already have a strong urge to devour you," he said slowly, in a whisper that rang through me.

Heat stroked my skin. My breaths shuddered at his voice. It was rough and smoky as he was, like a campfire burning low in the dark. This kind of interaction—the proposition of just sex—wasn't new to him, obviously, but it was to me. For years, I hadn't so much as looked at another guy with the potential of flirting, let alone…that.

I should be slapping him, throwing his drink in his face, getting up and leaving this place entirely, anything but soaking my panties, imagining this voice waking me up late on a Sunday morning for an early fuck.

He wasn't even a handsome man. His face could have been carved with a serrated blade. Too rough. Too bold. His hair and eyes were immensely dark now that the lights were to his back. All that blunt, craggy darkness made him look mean…and hot as sin. If he were written in a book, he'd be the villain.

The villain women like me fantasized about doing nasty things with. God knew I'd been devouring those books for years. Men always sounded better in romance. Even villains and monsters.

And the way he was looking at me... He was already devouring me.

His mouth curved up with a smirk. I didn't know if it was the dark, but I noticed he had no lines on his face whatsoever. He looked rather young, but not that young to have no smile lines or crinkles around his eyes. "How old are you?" I asked.

His smirk grew into a grin. Yeah, still no lines. It creeped me out. "Old enough to be here," he shook his glass, "drinking bourbon."

"Like twenty-one?"

"Way older." He tilted his head, looking me over. "You're rather sweet, lady in red who wouldn't tell me her name before asking about my age. You don't look like you come to these kinds of places very often."

Was it that obvious? "I'm not sure how to take that."

"As a compliment. You're the freshest thing in town."

"Well, well, I leave you alone for one second, and the wolves come down." Katrina returned with a tray of blue and purple drinks.

Thank God.

"You must be Katrina," he said, still eating me with his eyes.

I glanced up at my friend, who was reprimanding me with her glare. I returned a 'save me' stare.

She placed the tray on the table and cocked a brow at him. "You're in my seat."

"Apologies." He got up as if he had all the time in the world. Then he nodded at me once, slowly, his smile turning brighter. "Till we meet again. Happy birthday, Red."

CHAPTER 2

BELLE

Within minutes on the dance floor, I felt boneless, mindless and deliciously untethered.

Katrina moved around me, yell-sang the songs, blending in the mass of sweaty bodies around us.

I wanted my youth to linger a little bit. This was how I could have spent my early twenties: at clubs and frat parties, under the lights, dancing in a scrap of a dress, meeting men who wanted to devour me, watching my friends be wild and silly and young.

I didn't have to get married to an abusive motherfucker when I was twenty-one. I didn't have to get married at all.

For the love of me, I couldn't wrap my mind around how blind I had been. I chose that. I chose to be Professor Montgomery's wife. He was charming, not just for a professor. He dressed to the nines in suits and expensive shoes. He spoiled me, taking me to all these fancy restaurants, buying me ridiculously expensive gifts. And I was poor, with a scholarship I guarded with my life; I couldn't afford college any other way.

He took me in. Helped me with my studies. Convinced me I had to become a teacher and promised he'd be there every step of the way. I couldn't see his intention was to keep me under his eyes, all for him, at all times.

Back then, Declan was a dream come true for me, and for two years before we got married, I loved every part of us. I should have known then that behind that charming facade hid a monster.

It was the little things I should have paid attention to from the start, like the designer clothes and shoes he bought me. I was flattered and fucking happy, but then I realized he was trying to control what I wore, when I wore it and for whom. Then the control at school, picking my classes and friends for me, pushing away those who kept warning me about him.

I actually believed he was protecting me, and he was the only one who loved me more than anyone else in the world.

Until I had no one but him.

Everybody else thought I didn't want them in my life. Nothing could have been further from the truth. I was so alone and scared. My body wasn't mine anymore. It was his to do with what he wanted whenever he wanted. I was rape fucked, body, mind and soul, every day, and everybody thought I was a happy, snobby, gold digger bitch.

I stopped moving, tears pricking my eyes against my will.

"Hey, don't think," Katrina yelled over the music. "Just dance, birthday girl."

I nodded fast and lifted my chin to the playful lights so my tears wouldn't spill. I danced my heart out, telling myself it wasn't too late. I was twenty-eight today. Life was still ahead of me. Katrina was a living, bouncing example I could still learn to live and enjoy life.

Swirling, I met the dark eyes again. Just behind Katrina, set into the shadows off the dance floor, Alec stood, and neither of us looked away.

He was sipping his bourbon without a care in the world. I could tell by how unsurprised he seemed to be caught staring that he'd been watching my every move.

And he wanted me to know.

That was more potent than the blue and purple alcohol I'd downed earlier. It heated every inch of my skin, burned a hole deep down into my belly. It was dangerous in an exciting way.

A smile spread across my face as my arms stretched up to the ceiling. I could feel the hem of my dress inching up my thighs and didn't care. I wondered if he noticed.

I hoped he noticed.

Never in my life had I felt so hot, so completely in control of what I wanted; I wanted to dance like crazy with a smoldering stranger standing in the shadows, watching me.

"He's creepy but sexy as fuck," Katrina said. "And if his dick is as big as it looks in those pants, I say you give it a shot."

I slapped a hand over my gaping mouth. "You noticed that, too?"

"I'd be blind if I didn't."

"You're a happily married mom."

"Doesn't mean I don't have eyes…or a pussy."

I giggled like a girl old enough to be in my class. Then all the drinks I had hit me hard in the bladder. "I think I peed myself a little. I'll be right back."

As I stepped off the dance floor, weaving, her arm steadied me. "Do you need me to come with you?"

"No, keep dancing. I'll be back in a minute. Maybe order some more drinks?"

"All right. I'll tell them to have the cake ready, too."

I couldn't resist looking behind her to see if Alec was still there. But the shadows were dark and empty; he was no longer there watching me.

My stomach dropped as the fantasy was over. How long was it going to last anyway? I told the guy straight up I wasn't looking. And this was a nightclub packed with women who wanted to be picked up. Nobody waited for no one.

I followed the signs to the second floor, which was some sort of balcony overlooking the entire club. I walked down a narrow hallway and into a bathroom so bright that a pulse of pain spiked from my eyes to the back of my head.

Luckily, it wasn't crowded as I really needed to pee. On my way out, I fixed my hair and touched up my lipstick. The music downstairs felt like it was coming up from underwater.

I walked out of the door and right into a wall.

CHAPTER 3
BELLE

"Hello, Red."

My heart thrashed. We'd been close when he was standing at the booth, but not this close. Not my face to his throat, his smell of man and bourbon surrounding me. "Hi, Alec."

"You're a tiny, wild thing."

Tiny? That was a word that couldn't be used to describe me. I had big…everything. But…I liked it, coming from him. "I'm not wild."

"The way you dance begs to differ. I was watching."

"You're such a creep."

"Perhaps. But something tells me you liked being watched. By a creep like me."

My breath caught. My legs wobbled, like they weren't sure if they should run or collapse at his feet so he would pick me up in those huge arms. I chewed on my bottom lip, suppressing a smile.

He tucked my hair behind my ear, and a chill ran through me. "I still don't know your name."

"Red." I couldn't believe my voice right now. It was low and seductive and teasing. Who the fuck was I around this guy?

His eyes darkened even more. "I'm serious. I want to know everything about you."

"No, you don't. You just want to *devour* me."

His stare trained on me, turning my nipples into little rocks. "That, too."

He's creepy but sexy as fuck. And if his dick is as big as it looks in those pants, I say you give it a shot.
"Fine. My name is Belle."

"Belle?"

"Well, Isabella Ferro. But I had a French parent…" I fought the urge to say Professor. I gave him enough information for one night.

"Originally Italiana?"

I grinned. "Si, si."

"My favorite."

"To devour?"

He smirked. "Did you imagine I was getting hard watching you dance…Belle?"

"Wow." I gave up. I couldn't keep up with his directness. Had men like this always existed? "Were you …?"

He reached down, took my hand, and pressed it firmly to his erection, already arching into my palm.

A shiver took over me, and wetness gathered between my legs. He was really…long and thick and hard. I couldn't believe I was wondering about it an hour ago, and now it was in my hand.

Fuck.

Without thinking, I curled my fingers around him. "This is from watching me dance?"

"Do you always dance like this?"

If I hadn't been so astounded by him or the cock pulsing in my palm or this night in its entirety, I would have snorted a laugh. "Never."

He studied me, his eyes pensive. "Come home with me."

My head spun as I shook it. "No. There is

no way I'm leaving this club with you."

He bent and pressed a small, careful kiss to my neck. "You want me as much as I want you. I can feel your heat from here. Smell it. So why fight?"

The answer would take ten years of explanation.

Wait, what? He could feel my heat and smell me? I took a deep breath, and yeah, I could smell me, too.

Looked like there was no point in resisting.

Finally, I dragged my hand away from his erection, only to lead him past the restrooms farther down the narrow hallway to a tiny abandoned alcove overlooking the DJ station. It was secluded enough yet unhidden; if they would look up, anyone down there could see us through the glass wall.

I rested my back on it, my heart racing. "Okay. Touch me over here."

He raised an eyebrow, ran a long finger across my collarbone, from one shoulder to the other. "Here?"

My pussy clenched from the feeling of his calloused skin on mine. I was so hung up on the size of his cock that I'd failed to notice the size of his hands before.

God help me.

Big cock. Big hands. Sexy as sin body and

voice.

That was some package to belong to one man. A dangerous one that got me dropping all my guards for one night of long awaited pleasure.

I promised myself I'd start living all what I'd missed and not waste any more time. Let it begin.

What harm could come from one wild night anyway?

"Yes, here." I pressed my hand below his ribs. What the hell was he made of? This firmness couldn't be real. "You're not an abusive, narcissistic, psycho motherfucker, are you?"

Laughing, he bent and stared into my eyes. Then he plunged his fingers into my hair. "I am many things, but not that, no."

"Good." I reached up, wrapped a hand around the back of his neck, and pulled him toward me for a kiss.

Why I was about to kiss a total stranger, ditching my only friend who was probably eating my birthday cake all by herself now, eluded me. But she told me to give it a shot, right?

She didn't exactly mean I go fuck him across a wall where anyone could see, but I didn't care. In fact, I loved the new wild me. I could be that woman who enjoyed herself whenever, wherever, without shame or guilt.

A woman in control. A woman who was not afraid to take what she wanted and deserved.

His fleshy lips were blazing and hard on mine with the taste of bourbon adding to the warmness. He groaned when I opened my mouth and let him in.

That was exactly what I needed. Feral lust that sent a shiver through my whole body with just one kiss. And the heat I was now feeling from him, seeping through the soft fabric of his shirt, set me on fire.

A perfect start.

Declan never felt this hot while he touched me, even on the good days. He was never turned on by me or my body. He was aroused only by what he did to me, how he hurt me. The sense of power. I meant absolutely nothing to him. He'd have felt the same with anyone in my position.

But with this stranger I met a moment ago... He chose me of all the women in the place. He waited for me. He was turned on by me, burning for me.

I took his hand and brought it to my hip. "Can you really smell me?"

"Yes." His eyes glinted with something

savage. "It's driving me insane."

Moving his fingers to the edge of my dress, I whispered, afraid to sound silly instead of seductive, but I said it anyway. "Time to add a taste to the smell."

His gaze burned with golden strikes I hadn't seen before. "You really want me to do this here?"

The idea of giving myself to this man I knew nothing about, in this dark corner scared me. But there were many other things in the world that scared me a lot more. None of them felt as good as this one.

I nodded, my pulse throbbing between my legs.

His teeth scraped over his bottom lip in hunger. I could see he wanted to take a taste right here right now. To lift the hem of my dress and let me ride this big mouth. "You're much more trouble than I thought."

"Is that another compliment?"

His mouth curled, but need carved into his face as he leaned in and braced one hand against the wall. His fingertips on the edge of my dress teased the sensitive insides of my thighs. Then he lifted the red thing and slid his whole hand down my underwear. "Holy fuck. I was all set to get you riled up with my mouth, but you're already soaking."

I clenched hard, waves of heat engulfing me up and down.

"Let's get you out of that wet thing." He ripped my panties with one swift move.

I gasped. This panty-ripping thing needed a lot more strength than anyone would think, and it only happened in movies and books. But Alec did it…without a blink.

"I'll keep these." He shoved my underwear in his pocket before I could speak. "Now, let's get you even wetter." He got to his knees and ducked his head under my skirt. Then his tongue slicked through my wetness.

"Oh God." My hand banged the wall, the other gripped on his hair—wow. It was so soft and thick, just enough to dive in and grab.

Closing my eyes, toes curling in my pumps, I bit my lip as his tongue fluttered inside me. Then the realization I was exposed to anyone who would come to this area slapped me hard.

When Alec was standing against me, no one could see me but the people downstairs, who were too busy to look up. It was probably the only reason I went for…this.

He was big enough to protect me from people's eyes, maybe even from everything. I knew I was crazy. It could go both ways with a man this size; it could either be very dangerous or very safe, and for some reason, I did feel safe.

But now, any person walking here would see I was being…devoured.

My eyes snapped open. "Shit."

He pulled away and glanced up at me, my juices covering his chin. "Shit?"

I shook my head fast. "I didn't mean… It is so good, but… God, you look so hot covered in…me…"

He swiped his tongue over his lips, his eyes rolling back. "You taste so fucking good."

More drops trickled between my thighs as I pulled on his hair, squirming as his long finger replaced his tongue. "Oh my… Maybe you should come back up here. I'm not as wild as you think I am."

He looked over his shoulder as he got up, and then smirked at me as if he understood what was going in my mind. "Very well." His body pushed against mine, his finger slithering in my wetness, cock pressing to the side of my hip. "As much as I love your taste, I love you pressed to me like this even more."

His thick finger pushed deep, and I muffled a scream, pleasure spearing through me. He gave a hoarse grunt, and his arm snaked around my waist, pulling me even closer to him. With his weight braced on his forearm, he rested his forehead against mine, his breaths gusting over my lips.

For a moment, I was unaware of anything beyond his long finger sliding in and out of me. Then there were two.

Frantic need pulsed through my veins with every push and twist. My breasts swelled and pressed against his firm body. His cock was throbbing hard against me.

"So fucking tight." He gritted out, screwing his fingers into me. "I need to fuck you, Belle, and I need it now, but I'm afraid I might hurt you if I do."

"Not when I'm that wet," I said, too fast.

His teeth grazed along the side of my neck and down to my shoulder. They were rather sharp yet sending a sweet quiver of pleasure down my spine. "I could eat you up whole right now."

"You're such an animal." I laughed into his shirt, rocking against his hand.

He pulled his hand away, and I felt a chill where his warm fingers had been. Then his stare and jaws went hard.

Did I offend him somehow?

"But I like this raw, animalistic hunger," I amended. "It's so hot."

He dug into his pocket and pulled out a

tiny package. "Okay. Let's see if you can take every rough and filthy thing this animal does to your snug little pussy."

I gasped and clenched around the cold air, hating the emptiness. "Is that a condom? You just happen to have a condom in your pocket?"

It would never have occurred to me to bring a condom with me to some random club.

He just smiled and bent to kiss me. First softly, and then harder, hungrier. When my breath was too fast to catch, he wandered away, sucking at my jaw, my ear, my neck, where my pulse hammered wildly.

He touched my breasts, fondling them as our lips mashed, then he brought one out and feasted on my nipple.

"Oh my God, Alec. I can't take this. Please, don't make me wait any longer."

My dress had fallen back down my thighs, but he lifted it back up to my waist. His teeth clenched as his fingers dug into my bare ass pressed to the glass wall. "Pull my dick out, you wild thing."

I reached for him, shaking with the force of my own hunger. I tugged on the leather and let the buckle hang free. Then I attacked the snap of his pants. The weight of his cock did the rest, forcing the zipper down.

The hot, thick inches filled my hand, and I mentally tried to brace myself for what I'd gotten myself into.

It must have shown on my face because he laughed. "If you're having second thoughts, put it back inside, and I'll still make you come with my fingers and tongue. But once I'm inside you, it won't be easy to stop."

I measured his enormous length with a stroke that seemed to never end. He shuddered as my thumb brushed the slick tip. "You just have to prepare me for it, but I'll take it. Every inch."

He swore under his breath, the golden strikes flaming in his eyes again. I pushed his boxers down just enough for him to move and rubbed his erection across my opening.

A groan burst out of his throat. "Let me get this on." His hand left my ass as he ripped the package with his teeth. Then he rolled the condom on his hardness.

Without another moment of hesitation, he hefted me up, the friction of the glass against my back and ass an unexpected burn. When he lifted my leg, spreading me, I felt nothing but the thrill of having a man like that in a moment such as this.

He hooked my knee around his hip,

making me grateful for my heels. His gaze ripped away from my naked boob and burned into mine. "Someone could walk down here," he reminded me, and I became slicker. "You like that, don't you? You like that I'm gonna bounce these pretty tits out of this dress while I fuck you where anyone could see?"

A giggle of embarrassment and amusement flew out of my mouth. If I wasn't already on fire, I'd feel my cheeks burn. He was going to take me, right here, overlooking the crowd below, where Katrina—who knew me as a weak, shy pussy—was eating my birthday cake alone.

I was not a weak, shy pussy. Anyone who had to go through what I had to go through was not weak.

I was a survivor.

And definitely, after tonight, no one would call me—or my pussy—shy.

His breath hissed through his teeth as I guided him to my entrance, his shaft a hot throbbing heaviness I couldn't close my fingers around.

With his tip lodged inside me, he bared his teeth at me as he widened his stance and pushed inside me as slowly as possible.

My arms wreathed around his neck, shaking. I felt as if he reached my throat with his cock, and he wasn't all in yet. It didn't hurt, though. It was all a matter of pressure. Too much at first. I arched my back, tilting my hips to ease it, unable to stop the whine in my throat that melted with the deafening music. Then when his short thrusts stretched me and gained a steady rhythm, I got used to it.

He watched every reaction on my face with a smile, the golden strikes brighter than the strobe lights. I didn't think sex with strangers was supposed to be intimate like this. And deliciously scary.

The smile on his face was that of a beast about to *devour* me, but the tightness of his features showed a lot of restraint. He was struggling…not to tear me apart with his big big big cock?

My heart thrashed. Something about him right now, something primal triggered my instincts. But the pleasure he made me feel numbed it in a flash. If he were a serial killer about to slit my throat, I'd die a happy woman with a much wanted, big, fat cock in my pussy.

How many women could say that about the way they left this universe?

His head fell back as he slid deeper. "You're so fucking tight on my cock. So fucking good." His voice was tight, too.

I laughed at myself in my head. He wasn't a serial killer. He was just a man inside a pussy he liked.

His words fell away as he went deep inside me, here in this chaotic club with living, breathing lights and music pulsing all around us, where people walked twenty feet away.

My entire world reduced to the place where he filled me, where he rubbed firmly against my clit with every stroke, where the warm skin of his hips pressed to my thighs.

I never thought I could be filled and stretched like that. I didn't know a man could burn for a woman like that.

There wasn't any more talking, only his groans echoing off the ceiling. His small strokes grew deeper, faster, and harder until he was all in. His teeth pressed into my neck, biting me a little too sharply, and I gripped his shoulders afraid I might fall.

"Every inch. Fuck," he said in disbelief, his voice hoarse on my neck, the buckle of his belt jingling and clinking with his thrusts. "You're tight but big, too. I love that."

I have a big pussy.

Is that the same thing as when a man has a big cock? Should I be proud of it? Brag about it among my friends— when I have some? Should I be telling that to other random men I will be fucking in clubs from now on?

I moaned a laugh. Having a big pussy felt like a riot. So hardcore.

Thank you, Alec.

He groaned like I was the best thing that ever happened to him, pushing against me, rocking me into the wall with my *big pussy* crammed full.

My tits bounced out of my dress as he promised. I tried to tilt my hips again so I'd free a hand for a second to send them back home, but his weight had me locked down tight to that wall. He rolled his hips, his full length reaching every muscle and fold inside, and pleasure bloomed deep. Clasping around him, I felt like I was about to explode.

A growl that almost sounded like a howl ripped out of his expanding chest. He slammed his hips forward, shunting his cock to the max. His groans and the wet slaps joined the jiggling buckle and the vibrating music. I screamed, pleasure rippling through me, blinding me with the sheer intensity.

For the first time in forever, I didn't feel the endless pain or emptiness or misery. All I felt was the joy and satisfaction of watching this huge stranger break with the pleasure I was giving him. Of orgasming to a man who didn't abuse me to get his rocks off.

Yes, I was coming. I'd forgotten how that felt. To come by a man's cock. I'd been denied the pleasure for years. How could I have come with an asshole like Declan? But Alec… He did the job in one night.

The swelling pressure tightened unbearably. My fingers twisted and curled in his hair, around his neck and into his shirt. Anywhere I could get my grip onto.

He lifted my other leg, wrapping both around his waist, and picked up the speed. Fast and urgent, he let out loud, raw grunts, elongating my orgasm.

His hips grew jagged and rough. I thought he might bruise me. *I hope he bruises me. I'll have a good one for a change.*

"Holy fuck." He exploded inside me, fingers digging hard into my ass. His spurts felt hot even inside the condom. And God, there were a lot.

This was the best sex of my life. Katrina would be proud of me.

I dared look behind his shoulder to see if anyone was approaching. For a second, I thought I was imagining things and my vision was affected by all the sweat and shortage of breath, because, for the love of me, I saw Alec's face at the end of the dark hallway.

I blinked and pulled Alec off my neck to take a good look at him—and to stop this biting thing he kept doing. It was hot at first, but now it was harboring on annoying. His teeth were really big and sharp.

"Are you all right?" He rolled his upper lip under his teeth.

"Yeah. I think I'm a little tipsy, though. High on booze and risque sex." I chuckled. "A moment ago I was seeing two of you."

He didn't laugh or seem to be surprised. His body went rigid, and he just stared at me.

"What? I'm fine." I reached for my boobs. Time to stow them back where they belonged. My eyes glanced behind his shoulder one more time.

I flinched, gasping, my boobs jumping with me, all my blood rushing away from my body.

Alec's face was still there in the dark, and it was coming our way.

CHAPTER 4
BELLE

"Hunting alone, Brother?"

"Brother?" I yelped, shaking my head like an idiot at the double Alec's faces, before my mind started working again. I hated when fear hijacked my brain like that. I might be book smart, but in frightening life situations I was a donkey in heels. "Oh…yeah…of course. That makes much more sense."

"Belle, this is my twin asshole, Kayden." Alec glared at his brother. "Asshole, Belle."

"Nice to meet you, Belle." Kayden's stare trained on me, up and down, back and front. "You're a fine woman."

I opened my mouth with a silent scream as I remembered my boobs and ass were hanging out, and Alec's cock was still inside me.

"Don't be a dick." Alec's hand tugged my breasts inside quickly, and then lowered my dress to cover my ass.

Kayden shrugged. "What? It was a compliment."

"What are you doing here?"

"What am I doing here? What are you doing here, Alec?"

I cleared my throat. "I don't mean to interrupt, but could you…?" I pointed down frantically, sweating in shame.

Alec stared at me in confusion.

Seriously? "It's not very nice to have an argument with another person while you're still…in…"

"Oh." He scowled, looking where our bodies were still connected. "Yeah, sorry." He began to withdraw out of me slowly and gently, and I hissed.

"I salute you." Kayden's jaw flexed at me. "Not many women can take—"

"Don't look!" Alec yelled, finally out of me.

"Please. It's not like you've grown something extra." Kayden smiled at me. "We have the same exact dick, in case you're wondering."

"Oh my God," I squealed. First because the sudden void Alec's cock left after such a stretch was really painful and searing. And second because I didn't need to have this image Kayden bluntly put in my head.

Or did I?

My gaze dropped to the thick erection Alec still had jutting from a tangle of dark hair. As he rolled off the condom, the swollen inches glistened, long and too big to imagine how he'd just been inside me.

"I really have a big pussy."

"Oh, okay. So you have no problem taking the two of us?" Kayden asked.

Declan should have really killed me that night. Did I blurt out stuff I wasn't supposed to out loud? Again?

My jaw tired of hanging, I just laughed and unhooked my legs from around Alec.

"You are really an asshole, you know that?" He snarled at his twin. Then he helped me off the wall and steadied me with his elbow as my legs wobbled to the floor.

I smoothed my dress down and took a deep breath of sultry air. "All right. Thank you, Alec, for the… It was…" I pressed the tips of my thumb and index finger together as if I was complementing a chef on a delicious dish. My eyes barely met Kayden. "Nice to meet you, too, Alec's twin." My feet rushed backwards. "Now, if you'll excuse me, gentlemen, while I go do the walk of shame."

"Belle, wait," Alec called after me, but I'd already twisted and scampered to the end of the hallway.

His shouts died behind with the music once I flew down the stairs and elbowed my way through the dancing crowd. Luckily, Katrina was still in our booth—I thought she would have left by now, thinking I'd ditched her.

I grabbed her hand and dragged her out. "We have to go. Now."

CHAPTER 5

ALEC

Kayden drove us in silence all the way to the woods west of Forest Grove, but I could hear every growl rumbling in his chest.

I rolled down the truck window and tilted my face into the wind. My lungs filled with the pure air of the wilderness night. We were a few miles from the creek where I usually ran. Taking a bigger whiff, I caught the smell of damp leaves, squirrels, Garter snakes…and her.

Belle's fragrance and taste lingered on my skin, and even the woods wouldn't overpower them. It didn't help that I carried her wet panties in my pocket. Damn. That smell must have been filling Kayden's nose all along.

The asshole wanted her. He never said it, but he didn't need to. That was why he'd kept his big mouth shut since we left the club. No scolding, no warnings. The hell, I expected a bone-shattering fight, and he gave me nothing.

Yet.

Once he settled his inner struggle, applying his moral code to whatever he was feeling, he would start with me.

Well, I didn't blame him. But what was I supposed to do? I bet if he'd been the one there all night, smelling her, hearing her heartbeat, watching her dance, he would have forsaken everything he'd been preaching and sunk his teeth in her already.

Who wouldn't want a woman like Belle? She looked so damn good. Shiny black hair I loved messing up with my big hands. Hazel eyes burning with life itself. A cute little nose I wanted to rub my big one on over and over. A mouth… Oh, God, those lips…

And that was just her face.

Her body was a different story. That pussy

of hers…would start wars.

I hissed as I recalled the feeling of her tightening around my cock, the memory set my balls aching.

I really need a run.

"The fuck? Isn't it enough what you've done? You're thinking about her cunt right here next to me?" Kayden grumbled.

"What the… How did you know?"

"You're making sex sounds!"

"No, I'm not!"

"Yes, you are." He pointed at my thigh with his whole hand. "And look at that. Your dick is digging a hole in your pants."

"Why are you looking at my dick, you perv?"

He swerved the truck and stopped it off the trail. "I'm the perv? I'm the one who couldn't keep it in my pants until we sorted things out?"

I rolled my eyes. "Kayden, don't go all alpha on me now. Belle is mine"

"No. She belongs with the pack, yes, but she was not yours to claim." He killed the engine. "Not yet anyway. She has a choice to make before she even picks a mate."

"She always chooses me. Why do you think it's going to change this time?"

"Not always. And if you were so sure she

would, why didn't you wait?"

I stormed out of the truck and slammed the door behind me. "I'm going for a run."

Another door slammed shut. "I'm coming with you."

"No. I want to be alone." Snapping at the buttons of my shirt, I kicked off my shoes. "And she will choose me."

He leaned against the hood and crossed his arms over his chest. "I don't know about that. You spooked the fuck out of her."

"Me? *You* spooked the fuck out of her, showing up like that, eating her up with your eyes." I unbuckled the belt and dropped my pants. "We were doing great until the 'you're a fine woman' speech." I thickened my voice in the end, mocking him.

"I showed up to stop you, but I was too late. Do you have any idea how we're going to explain all that shit to her in the morning? To the bears?"

"The bears don't have to know. They never wanted to have anything to do with that witchy deal we made anyway."

"We all belong to the same twin shifter pack. Don't ever forget that, Alec. They're our brothers, and it's their right to know what happened."

I shrugged off my shirt, opened the door to

the truck and piled all my clothes in the front seat. Rage surged through my veins, and I could feel the beast banging loose. "Do whatever you have to do, Alpha. All I care about is getting Rena back."

"Belle. This one's name is Belle," he corrected. "If we had a fifty-fifty chance to win her over, now it's one in a million. Well done, Bro."

My fists clenched hard. I hated it when he was right. I fucked up. I knew I did. But I wouldn't admit it. Not to him.

"At least, tell me you didn't ruin that one chance and bit her already."

I slammed the door shut again, scowling at him. "Of course not."

His stare pinned me down. "You sure? Your face was buried deep in her neck."

And I nibbled at that. She tasted so fucking good, and holding back was not easy. "I mean…I did bite her but not like that."

"You motherfucker," he seethed.

"I did not turn her, Kayden."

He growled, kicking at the ground. Then he tore at his shirt through the swirl of twigs and leaves he made. His beast was banging loose, too. "Let's hope for your sake before anyone else's you didn't."

CHAPTER 6
BELLE

A roar I did not recognize, more like a wailing siren, woke me up. It took me a moment of fighting through the headache squashing my skull to realize I was hearing my alarm going off.

The red numbers flared at my half-open eyes. 6:30.

How could it be morning so fast?

I turned it off and was about to press a pillow over my head and go back to sleep when I realized it was my first day at school.

Fuck. I bolted upright and leapt to my feet,

my head and eyes screaming and screeching in pain. The bedroom was all sunshine. That never went well with hangovers.

Note to self: bay windows are awesome and everything but buy double sided blackout curtains next time.

I quickly grabbed my gray suit from the closet, set it on the bed and headed to the shower. I wasn't going to let anything ruin my first day of class. Not my wild adventure last night or this nasty hangover.

I jumped in the shower and let the warm water drift over me. The image of my huge stranger wouldn't leave me be. Everything we'd done was still fresh in my mind. So vivid. So real.

Even his smell was still on me.

My pussy throbbed, sore yet aching for more Alec.

Who would have thought me, the abused Professor from the Beauty and the Beast case—*cheesy, I know. Belle who fell for the beast?*—that was all over the news for the past few months, was going to meet a very hot stranger at a club and decide right away to have sex with him in public?

What in the hell had gotten into my head when I dragged Alec to that corner?

That was one intense fuck, though.

I wouldn't mind if it happened again.

Despite everything, last night was wonderful. I lost myself to my desires, and it felt so good. The ability to make a choice, even if it was a mistake. To take a calculated risk, knowing it could go both ways and accept either result.

No one was forcing me to do anything last night.

That alone was a blessing.

Of course, everything had turned awkward when the twin saw me naked, screwing his brother, and I ran off without knowing anything about my stranger except his first name.

It was for the best. To never see him again. It was a one night stand. It was safer to keep it that way.

I needed to focus on my new life and job. I couldn't wait to stand in a classroom again.

Be me again.

My phone rang as I stepped out of the shower. I wrapped a towel around my body and walked out of the bathroom. The cool air felt chilly on my wet skin. Despite the sun, this was still Oregon. I wasn't used to the weather here yet; it was a far stretch from California.

I picked up the phone. It was Katrina.

"Hey, you naughty, naughty girl," she said. "How's it going?"

I chuckled. "Great. I…was getting dressed."

"Puking yet?"

"Nope, I'm good. Super excited."

"Good to hear that. The first day is always rough, but remember it's the first day of the year for everybody. So don't let the kids see you sweat."

"I won't," I said. I really wasn't nervous. I loved being a teacher, and inside the classroom I was a completely different person. Assertive. Comfortable. Happy. It was where I belonged.

"Okay. You sound so…prepared. I guess I was all worked up for nothing."

"I can be a little nervous for the sake of your maternal instincts if you want."

"Nah, don't worry about it. You're a grown ass woman. You don't need my overprotective blah blah blah, whatever you call that in your Psychology course. But thank you for offering."

I ruffled my wet hair, moving toward the mirror. "Any time. What time are you leaving?"

"In a couple of hours."

"You sure you can't stay for a day or two?"

I'd have loved to have one friendly face to hang out with while I got used to this new town.

"I wish. But hubs has already lost it with the kids. I have to rescue them." She laughed. "Halloween is only two months away, though. I'm visiting again then."

"Halloween? Why on Halloween?"

"Oh, Forest Grove throws the meanest Halloween parties every year. The best in all Oregon and Washington combined. I wouldn't miss it for anything." She paused. "Okay, hubs is on the other line. I got to go. Knock 'em dead today."

"I will." I ended the call and went to find my blow dryer when I saw some discoloration on my neck. Did Alec do that?

Studying the little marks on my neck, I guessed it was from those little bites. Perfect. A hickie on my first day at school.

I removed the towel to check for any more bruises. It was a routine check for me years ago until I stopped examining my body. What had been the point of finding if I had new bruises or trying to hide or heal them? I'd have gotten more anyway.

Some yellowish spots were on my hips and butt. They were definitely from Alec's pressure. Evidence I didn't dream our quick adventure.

I smiled, ready for whatever other adventures this fresh start had for me.

CHAPTER 7
BELLE

The day was bright and beautiful as I drove to the campus. I grabbed my bag and hurried to get to Professor Pattison's office, the Psychology Head of Department. He was Katrina's acquaintance; the one who gave me the job. He knew all about Declan and was so supportive that he promised me a co-teacher for the first half of the semester until I regained my speed and found a TA.

I hadn't had the chance to meet my co-teacher yet because he was on a leave. But today, Professor Pattison was introducing us.

Once inside the building, I was transported to a world I'd missed for a whole year. A place full of hustling and bustling young people eager to learn…and have nonstop sex.

Grinning from ear to ear, I walked down the hallway and turned the corner till the very end where I found Professor Pattison's office.

"Professor Ferro." He greeted me with a firm handshake.

I might have returned the shake with a little too much enthusiasm. Being here, hearing that designation with my last name, not Declan's, made me so elated. By the look on his face and the way he withdrew his hand, I'd say I was too elated for my own good. *Tone it down, Belle. You don't want to come off as a nutcase.*

"Just in time." He gestured for me to take a seat. When I did, he adjusted his brown suit jacket and sat behind his desk, a formal smile on his clean-shaved face. I was surprised when Katrina told me he was around fifty-years-old. He looked too much younger to be even forty. His dark blond hair didn't have a hint of a single gray one or a receding line. He had sharp, green eyes, a healthy tan, a fit, tall body…I didn't get it. Should I ask him what his secret was or was that too much?

"I've just sent for Professor Asher, your co-teacher for the next few months," he said. "You will have to work together on a schedule and the rest of the arrangement. I decided it would be best to leave it to both of you because I'd like you to work at your own pace at first.

"I'm sure you'll find cooperating with Professor Asher to be an easy task. He is one of our finest, been working here for ten years, which means he knows everyone and can help you with anything you need around campus. Can I get you anything until he arrives?"

"Thank you. I've already had my coffee," I said. "I…can't thank you enough, though, for giving me this chance to work with you. I can't wait to start."

"It's our pleasure to have you, Professor."

Someone knocked on the door. Must be my new colleague. I hoped he wasn't a snob or a sleaze. Those were the worst in Academia.

My gaze shifted to the door as it opened. A man carrying a black briefcase that matched his suit took one step inside the office. Then his gaze fell on me, and he stopped in his tracks, his hand tightening around the knob.

Hello sexy, suave and sophisticated.

I always had a thing for professor glasses,

and young me thought Declan was sexy as hell with them on. Now, I hated everything Declan, but I still associated the glasses with sexiness in my subconscious.

And this man… He rocked them.

Didn't Professor Pattison say my co-teacher had been working here for ten years? That would make him in his forties, thirty-five, at least.

Well, that one looked much younger than that, even with the glasses. Maybe even younger than I was. How was that possible? What was it with the men here looking younger than they were supposed to be? There must be something in the water in Oregon.

Note to self: consider Botox, you wrinkly hag.

But it wasn't only the glasses or the slim fit suit on that body of an athlete, not a college professor, that held me in place, unable to move my eyes away from his face.

He had something else. Something…almost mesmerizing.

A rare masculinity that radiated from him in waves, pulling me to him against my will. His face too beautiful to be real. Even his scent warm and sensual in the strangest way.

I didn't like that.

I didn't like his charms having that crazy

effect on me. I'd just seen the man, and I was already fantasizing about doing nasty things I should never be doing to a colleague at a workplace, especially a prestigious university such as here.

"Come in, Joshua," Professor Pattison said.

Yes, come in, Josh-ooh-wah! Get inside. Break that awkward stare I can't bring myself to break. Please?

Why wasn't he moving? Why wasn't he looking away?

And…was that a good stare or a bad stare? Like 'you're so gorgeous I fell in love with you from first sight' stare? Or 'I hate your guts for no reason. I'm going to make your life a living hell then murder you in your sleep' stare?"

My heart was racing, my head spinning, but somehow, I was calm. There was something extraordinary about this man. Even if he was picturing how to snap my neck in his head, I felt soothed by his existence.

Professor Pattison cleared his throat. "Come meet the department's newest addition. Professor Isabella Ferro is going to be teaching here with us."

Joshua's head snapped toward him. It was a few moments before he finally left the doorknob, closed the door and walked to the seat before me.

I was going to extend my hand for a proper

greeting—not because I wanted to feel his wedding-band-free hand around mine or anything like that—but he wasn't even looking at me when he unbuttoned his jacket and sat. He set his briefcase on his lap, a deep grimace on his face, ignoring me completely.

"As I was saying, Professor Ferro will be teaching General Psychology and Abnormal Psychology this semester," Professor Pattison said.

"That's what I teach." Joshua's voice was deep and low, the kind that hit you right in the core and silenced you to listen.

"That's why I chose you to be her co-teacher for the first—"

"That's a terrible idea."

I cocked a brow, and then I looked at the Head of Department.

He fiddled with his tie, giving me another managerial smile. "Why would you say—"

"You really think I can work with her?" Joshua interrupted again.

Okay. Professor sexy, suave and sophisticated was officially a dickhead. At first, I thought this might be a payroll issue. Sharing classes could mean a deduction sometimes, which wasn't the case here. Professor Pattison assured me of that, and since that dickhead had just been informed, I thought that was his problem.

But then he spoke again, and apparently, the issue was that I had a vagina.

I couldn't remain silent anymore. "I'm right here, sitting across from you. I can hear everything you say."

"Good."

I gaped at him in disbelief. "Excuse you? If you have a problem with me in particular, Professor, say it. Do you even know me to not want to work with me?" Glaring at him, I grabbed my bag. "You know what? Forget it." I jumped to my feet. "Thank you so much, Professor Pattison, but I do not need a co-teacher. I'm fully capable of running my classes by myself."

"Nobody doubts that." My boss rose from his seat. "Could you please give us a minute, Professor?"

Fuming, I just stared at him.

He ushered me to the door, apologized on behalf of that asshole and asked me to wait outside.

I dropped on the couch in the waiting area, taking it out on my bag handle, shooting a death glare at dickhead Asher before Pattison closed the door.

What a way to start. One moment I thought the day was getting even better; how lucky I was that my co-teacher turned out to be pure hotness behind professor glasses. The next he crapped on my first day at work with his misogynist shit.

He takes one look at me, sees I'm a woman and decides I'm not good enough?

Men were pigs. All of them. I made the right decision when I swore them off for all eternity. Relationships with them…not their bodies. Those I could still use to my benefit. Last night was enough proof *just sex* was an outstanding arrangement. I'd be an idiot to give that up after years of—

The door opened, and the asshole burst out. "Let's go."

My face contorted in utter disgust. Who the hell did he think he was? He didn't even look at me, and he was already one stride away from leaving the office? "What the…"

"We have class in thirty minutes."

"If you think for one second that I will—"

"Look, I'm sorry."

That took me by surprise. I didn't expect a man like him to apologize, not this fast, not ever. I felt…betrayed. I wasn't ready to drop this feud yet. "Do not interrupt me, even if it is for an apology."

He twisted and stalked toward me, his gaze penetrating me now, unwavering like in those first seconds he'd laid his eyes on me. Was he going to give me more of his crap? I stood to level the confrontation. Bring it, asshole.

"Of course." He murdered my hopes at a decent verbal fight where I could blow all that steam stuffed in me. "I'd like you to know that was not my best behavior in there."

Are you shitting me right now? Where the fuck did that civil act come from? And what the fuck were those eyes made of? I'd never seen that color in my life. Grayish violet blue, like cold steel being shoved in a furnace.

Do not distract me with your beauty and sudden politeness. Return to the douchebag facade and let me have my payback, slashing you with my words. "You think?"

"Please accept my apology, and let's move on."

Fuck you. I folded my arms across my chest, my bag dangling down to my thighs. "And if I don't?"

"Then I'll keep on trying to apologize until you do, Professor Ferro." He gestured at the hallway. "Shall we?"

Fuck you one more time. How could I retort after this? The son of a bitch won with his eighteenth-century gentleman's talk, and all I was fighting now was a smile.

Professor Pattison emerged. "What's it

going to be, Professor Ferro? As much as I'd love for the two of you to work together, the decision remains yours."

CHAPTER 8
JOSHUA

It had never failed to amaze me how she looked exactly the same, moved the same, spoke the same.

Every time.

The spitting image of my beloved Rena. My destiny. My eternal dream.

Even her smell, the one that haunted me and made my mouth water with her every move, and the rhythm of her pulse that echoed through my dead chest.

The heart that soon would stop beating like

mine.

I walked by her side down the hallway, holding my fake breath. No more risks. I'd done enough damage for one day.

Despite her approval of Pattison's arrangement, she must be wondering why I acted the way I did in his office. With that glimpse of fire in her spirit she showed me, I had no doubt she would demand an explanation. I would have to come up with a convincing lie for now. She wouldn't be able to swallow the truth without a slow introduction.

"Are you being forced into this?" Her elegant neck stretched as she threw me a look from the corner of her eye.

I couldn't keep my stare away from the two veins bulging next to her throat, summoning all my willpower not to remind myself of her sweet taste.

She suddenly stopped and twisted at me. "Why do you keep staring at me like that? I don't like it."

I blinked, dragging my gaze away from her. "I'm not being forced."

She shook her head and resumed walking. "Then why did you change your mind all of a sudden? You don't expect me to believe you spent two minutes with Pattison and came out a changed man for no good reason."

"Damien Pattison is a very persuasive man. He put everything into perspective for me."

She narrowed her eyes. "And why did you say you didn't want to work with me in the first place? You don't even know me."

"I do," I murmured.

She stopped again. "What did you just say?"

"I do know you," I said firmly. "You're Belle…from the Beauty and the Beast case?"

Her face blanched, her long, black lashes fluttering. "How did you know about that?"

"The news."

Her chest rose with a deep breath, and flashes of all the things I'd once done with those breasts raced in my mind. "I didn't think my life had been a gossip material in Oregon, too."

"It must have been so hard for you that you had to move."

"You have no idea." She sighed. "Could you please not…share this piece of information?"

"Of course."

"Thanks." The rhythm of her heartbeat quickened as she clutched her bag. "But what has that got to do with anything? I mean… Wait a minute. I know what this is about."

Her brows shot up, and her stance changed from vulnerable to fierce in a split-second. "You think he's innocent. You empathize with the man that ruined my life."

She went on and on with her accusations. In no time, the conversation turned into a women's right argument and I was, apparently, mansplaining her.

I didn't interrupt because it seemed to have irritated her earlier…and because I thought the redness crossing her cheeks when she was angered was utterly cute.

"I know your kind, Professor," she said it as a warning.

"My kind?"

"A charming man like you, staff and students must be swooning over you all the time, practically throwing themselves at you. You think you're entitled to anything with any woman, and they have no right to open their mouths."

"These are very serious accusations, Professor Ferro. If I didn't know you were projecting, I'd be gravely offended."

She scowled and continued down the hallway until we reached my office. Damn, even her scowl was cute.

We stood at my door, and I rearranged my lies—half-truths. I was a quick and skilled liar, out of necessity and long experience. My expansive studies in Psychology helped as well. "Your assumptions about me are completely wrong, by the way. The reason I didn't want to spend a lot of time working with you is that your face is too much of a trigger for me."

"Trigger?"

"You remind me of someone, Professor. A woman who suffered like you. I was supposed to save her, but I couldn't." That part was true. Had my heart been still beating, it would have been ripped to shreds just at the memory.

Her big eyes grew to the size of dinner plates, yet her lips parted in the most attractive way. I wished I could have closed the distance between us and crushed my mouth to hers. "Now I feel like an asshole," she whispered.

"I beg your pardon?"

She did that thing with her thumbnail, a press on top that seemed painful but wasn't, followed by the run of her hand through her hair, Rena did every time she was embarrassed or nervous. "I did make assumptions way too quickly, and I misjudged you. I can't apologize enough…" She swore under her breath.

Rena didn't swear at all, but this one… I

found it intriguing. There was a fierce glow to Isabella, a life force that I hadn't seen in a long time. Something I'd long missed.

"You don't need to apologize. I deserved it," I said. "Besides, you think I'm charming."

Her struggle to hide her smile was adorable. She was adorable. Isabella.

My Isabella.

Her heart strutted. "If I am that much of a trigger, you really shouldn't be around me." She played with her hair again. It moved off her neck, and I could see what she'd carefully hidden with makeup.

A surge of fury blazed inside me, and I yearned to tear someone's flesh, gulp on their blood until they were dry. Wrath was the enemy of any vampire. The only thing that tampered with my control and threatened to expose me.

When did that happen, Isabella? How?

"Are you all right?" she asked, concern lacing her voice.

"Perfectly. As for your question, I'm going to see you here every day anyway. Might as well replace negative memories with positive ones with you."

This time, she smiled. A full grin with teeth. Hell, I'd missed that beauty so much. "You have a point. Good thing I don't need saving. Not anymore."

Oh, you're so innocent, my sweet Isabella. You have no clue what you've gotten yourself into.

But have no fear. I'm here to protect you, and I won't let anyone take you from me ever again.

CHAPTER 9
BELLE

I audited as Joshua started the first General Psychology lecture of the semester. I could feel the college sexual energy swirling around the auditorium. It was packed with students, mostly females, and I wondered if Psychology had become a popular major in the past year I had been forced out of Academia.

Or was it the Psychology teacher that was popular?

The answer came when I noticed several of

the students were staring at Joshua, hypnotized. Flirtatious smiles. Cute lash batting. Girlfriend snickers.

Yeah, it was definitely the teacher.

I had always been fascinated by the way we communicated with pheromones. Our first instinct toward the opposite sex was to size them up for mating or procreation, sending them a message of our appraisal through body odor.

We were humans, yet deep inside we were all basically animals, fueled with need, trying to survive.

Joshua went through with the lecture, ignoring the lustful glances, and the overacted giggles that burst every time he made a Psychology inside joke.

I, too, ignored it for my sanity. Although the physical attraction I had for Professor Asher was undeniable, our relationship had to be strictly professional.

I really shouldn't be involved with another professor for obvious reasons. Besides, there was no way I could compete with all these beautiful, young women crushing on him. I was way out of my league here. It'd been so long since I'd been in the game. Except for my students, I'd long forgotten exactly how to be around…people, not just men.

My total fuckup with Joshua was enough proof.

What was I thinking throwing judgments right and left, accusing a man I'd just seen of being another monster like Declan?

Note to self: even if you've suffered, you have no excuse to be a bitch.

Second note to self: it's time to start healing...for real.

I couldn't let Declan control me anymore. This grip he had on my mind had to be removed. Broken. Sooner than later.

Joshua glanced at me with a hint of a smile every now and then as if making sure I was all right. I hoped it was only a professional gesture, and he, too, wasn't projecting. I could see it in his eyes, a protective urge of sorts induced by his earlier trauma. I didn't want to pry earlier or even ask about the kind of trigger he mentioned. Psychosis? Substance abuse? Self-harm?

It could be many things, and they were all unpleasant. Nothing I'd want to be a part of.

But…

As much as I hated the effect Joshua had on me—and the effect I might have on him—part of me wanted to extend it as long as possible. I felt timid and uneasy around him yet intrigued. I had this feeling a man like him saw the world differently; he would show me the world in a way that I never knew existed. For some reason beyond all logic, even if he was screaming trouble, I believed I'd be safe if he was just there.

The lecture concluded. On the next one, it was his turn to audit, and mine to do what I was born to do.

I made my way to the front of the auditorium and sat my bag on the desk. Then I walked up to the white board and wrote my name. Professor Ferro.

Not Professor Montgomery.

I couldn't help the grin on my face or the tears forming in the corners of my eyes as I watched my name up there.

For the first time in what had seemed to be forever, I was me.

Everything I'd worked really hard for, everything I'd cried and sweated and bled for had come true today.

Turning to see the young faces heading my direction, I didn't think I'd ever been happier.

The looks from the male students reminded me of the steamy glances Joshua was receiving earlier from the girls. A myriad of emotions hit me at once. The satisfaction of feeling attractive to eighteen or nineteen-year-olds. It made me feel beautiful and desired even if I'd never act upon such taboo flirtation in any way. Then a certain memory crept to the back of my head and clawed at my heart.

It was my first month as a professor. One of my students had been giving me the 'I have a crush on you' face, yet he'd been so polite and never crossed the boundaries I'd carefully set. Until one day, I showed up with a split lip. He approached me after class, his eyes soft, his young face all determination and concern.

"I can help you," he had urged.

He was so innocent. I lied to push him away, but there had already been rumors. I thought I hid the bruises well. It turned out Declan had been bragging to his friends about the things he did to me.

When lying didn't work, I begged. I knew if Declan saw him, it would be the end of the boy's future. And Declan always watched. He had eyes on me everywhere.

The door to the classroom had opened just then, and my monster of a husband was there. My heart sank when my student spun and stood in front of me like he could save me.

I had been so afraid Declan would physically hurt the boy. But all Declan had done at that moment was hide behind a psychopath's sickening smile and linked arms with me, escorting me out.

At home, he broke my jaw that night. And the next day, my student was expelled.

I took a deep breath, hoping Declan was getting his ass kicked every night in jail. Then I dismissed all the negative thoughts and bad memories, nudging myself back to present time. There were no monsters here to bury me in fear. No one was going to get hurt because some psycho thought he owned me. I was safe, and so were my students.

I was safe. I repeated it over and over in my head like a sacred mantra.

And with Joshua in the room, I felt even safer.

"Good morning, class." That was all it took for confidence to wash over me as if I'd never been hurt or crushed once. "My name is Professor Isabella Ferro, and I'll be your General Psychology teacher this semester."

CHAPTER 10
BELLE

Joshua led me to the food court, a wince on his face as if he was constipated. "You were amazing up there."

"Thank you…I guess."

"You guess?"

"Well, your facial expressions rarely match your words. You look like you're in physical pain while complementing me."

The line between his brows deepened. "That's not… I really meant what I said."

"Yet you're still frowning." I glanced away from him as we reached the barista counter. Two more seconds and I'd be drowning in those eyes and forbidden fantasies I should have never pictured. "Can I get you anything?" *You could use some fibers.*

"Lunch is on me," he said it as a statement. Then he ordered before I could even respond.

Again, I didn't like that. The last thing I wanted was someone making choices for me, taking control of any aspect of my life without permission. "Shouldn't you at least ask me what I'd like to have?"

His face eased a little. "If you don't like it, you can always order something else, but I have a feeling I've guessed your preferences correctly."

"Do you now?" I was too angry to listen while he'd talked to the barista. There was no way he could have guessed what I liked to eat, though. I hated food everybody loved like mayo, eggs and onions. And for coffee, I only drank a cup in the morning. Anything more than that and I'd never sleep.

She returned with my lunch tray, reciting the order back. "One honey cinnamon tea, one turkey sandwich no onions or mayo, and a blueberry muffin."

What the hell? "Yes," I uttered,

dumbfounded.

"Did I get it right?" Joshua asked.

I cocked a brow at him, and he was smirking. "In the creepiest way ever."

His smirk turned into a smile for the first time. I could see now why he didn't do it so often. He looked like a predator that had just cornered a prey. His eyes moved up and down my body slowly, and eventually settled on my eyes, as if he was seeing me from the inside out.

Creepy, and a bit inappropriate. But for whatever reason, not only had I accepted it, but also I wanted more of it.

My mind was screaming, yet my body was betraying every ounce of lucidity in me. Thank goodness for padded bras; my nipples were pointing directly at him like little bullets ready to be shot at his mouth.

I loved to see him looking at me, fully digesting me. So primal, so untamed.

Then his smile vanished. "I thought you were joking, but it looks like I really scared you."

That's what he got from my staring? I really need to work on my horny looks.

"I'm not scared of you, Professor Asher." My voice fell at the end, and the way I said his name sounded like something naughty I'd call him while he was on top of me, tying my wrists.

Seriously, Belle. Stop it.

With shaking fingers, I reached for the tray, but his hands were faster. I gasped at the brush of his accidental touch. His fingertips were so cold, yet they sent a jolt of heat through me that made me shiver some more.

"Allow me." He carried the tray, unbothered, like nothing happened.

"Thanks." I sighed, ambling to a free table. We sat across from each other. He took off his glasses for a second to clean them with his tie.

Damn, those eyes. That was too much beauty for one person to have. I dropped my gaze, and it landed on his lips.

This is ridiculous. I give up.

How was I supposed to fight the temptation when he had all this? The smell, the face, the gaze, the lips, the body, the voice, the way he carried himself, the fucking glasses, even his name. I was crushing on Professor Asher whether I liked it or not. Hard.

With him around, my new life was not going to be as easy as I thought it would be.

I tore open the plastic case of my sandwich and munched on it like a starving animal, not bothering with how I must have been looking to him right now. My gaze wandered to the floor-to-ceiling windows of the food court, taking the view of the surrounding woods and the gray sky. It was very odd how the weather changed so rapidly around the day here. One minute it was sunny, the next it was dreary. Just like the emotions this man, watching me with intent interest while I was stuffing my mouth with turkey, struck in me.

"Aren't you going to eat anything?" *Please. Do anything awkward or ugly or disgusting. You're a man. It's not going to be this hard.*

"I had a big breakfast," he said. "Also, I prefer decent meals that aren't microwaved. If you'd like, I can show you the finest of Forest Grove's grills when you have the time."

I listened, lost in the depth of his voice. At times, he seemed to have an accent that I couldn't place, but then he'd speak again, and it would be gone.

Also…was he asking me out?

Not prepared for such question, I pressed hard on my thumbnail, a bad habit I had since I was a child, and later I changed into an anchoring technique to tone down anxiety. "Where are you from?"

"Oregon."

"Really?"

"Is that so strange?"

I shrugged, scarfing down the last bite of my sandwich. "I thought I detected an accent and sometimes you speak like you came out of Persuasion."

He put his glassed back on. "I reckon I just like Austen."

Give me a break. "You? You like Jane Austen."

"Actually, Persuasion is one of my favorites."

My nose crinkled. "I hate that book. Why would anyone like that book?"

His jaw flexed, and his gaze seemed distant. "I like it because time didn't get in between. They waited for each other, and in the end they got their happily ever after."

A fucking brooding, helpless romantic! A tormented soul with a broken heart! Oh, please. Just drop down your pants and put it in my mouth.

"What seems to surprise you, Professor?"

"You." I gulped on my cinnamon tea. Ummm...so good. "Contradiction after contradiction, it's giving me a whiplash." *And big gushes between my legs. I really need to change my panties.*

"I only contradict what you expected. Perhaps you just need to put all your assumptions aside and give yourself a chance to know who I really am. Then make your judgment, if you must."

He won again. I ran a hand through my hair, pressing my nail on the other. "You're right."

Now, he was surprised. "That's new."

"What is that?"

"A woman telling a man he's right."

I laughed under my breath. "If you stick around long enough, I might contradict your expectations too, Professor."

"I should take my own advice then."

The rest of the cinnamon tea flushed my cheeks with its tender warmth. "Would you mind if I start the next class? I know we don't have a plan or a schedule yet, but until we do, I want to be teaching it."

"I…" He frowned, his Adam's apple bobbing with a swallow. "I think it might be best if I did."

"No way. Abnormal Psychology is my jam. I've been looking forward to this class all day." I left my seat. When he didn't get up or relax his face, I raised a brow. "Unless you think I can't handle a senior class?"

"You know I don't," he said, rising to his feet. "You really need to stop using that defense mechanism every time you want something."

I rolled my eyes, a sheepish smile sneaking up on me. "I know. I'm sorry."

"No need to apologize. I…" He held my gaze in a way that took my breath away. "Please understand that I can't help but to feel very protective of you."

His words—and voice— toyed with my emotions. I felt on display under the intensity of his gaze. My tongue darted to lick my lips compulsively. So I turned to biting them and realized that this was also awkward. I was suddenly very aware of every single little gesture I was making, and my thumbnail didn't survive my attack.

The pain yanked me out Joshua's trance, bringing me back to reality. "Because of…my face?"

His lips twitched. "Of course. What else?"

Yeah, what else? So wake up, Belle. Wake the fuck up. The only reason behind his interest in me was that I reminded him of someone else.

I plastered the best fake smile I could muster. "Is there something particularly dangerous about the next class?"

Here came that wince again. There was something troubling this man more than he was sharing, and I'd be lying if I said I wasn't worried. It was understandable he wouldn't spill his guts to a stranger he'd just met. But I had a bad feeling about whatever he was hiding. As if…it had something to do with me, Belle, and not just an old trauma.

"No," he said in surrender. "I only thought you might want to slow down, take it easy on your first day."

I shook my head, frustration dulling my senses. "Well, I don't. But thank you for your concern." I started out of the food court.

He followed in silence until we reached 402B. It was a classroom, much smaller than the auditorium. Reluctantly, he took a seat, asking me with his eyes if I would change my mind.

I ignored him and tried to ignore the feelings that were punching my guts now. The students piled into the class, and I watched with growing interest, the negativity sifting away bit by bit.

This, standing up here, was all I needed for life to be good again. I didn't need a man. I didn't need to slow down. I didn't need to break my nails. I needed to teach. I had to teach.

When I thought everyone was there, I started to speak. But then I saw two more students walk in.

My heart skipped a beat then hammered against my ribs. My skin went ice cold then searing hot. I felt like I was going to pass out, like I was dying and my whole life was flashing before my eyes.

Or so I hoped.

Shoot. Me. Now.

Please.

It was them. Alec and his twin. The man—BOY—I fucked against a wall and his twin brother who watched. Right here in my classroom. As my students. Staring right through me.

Sick to my stomach, I wanted to bolt, to run outside that door they had just come through, screaming at the top of my lungs a big fat FUCK. But my feet were glued to the floor.

No amount of fingernails or classes was enough to take away the deep shit I was in.

CHAPTER 11
ALEC

Stupid! Stupid! What was I thinking?

I grumbled at myself as I stormed out of the campus with Kayden, following Belle's scent.

We'd gone to see her in her office after the lecture, but she wasn't there. I'd tracked her everywhere on campus, and when I couldn't find her, I sprinted outside, leaving the truck behind. I probably should have taken it to track her faster, but I was too angry with myself.

The look on her face when we entered the class would haunt me for the rest of...for the rest of the time we were allowed together.

I'd done something highly inappropriate and very dangerous. For her. For us. Kayden was right. I might have ruined my chances with her this time.

What had I been thinking following her to the club last night? Talking to her? Fucking her against a fucking wall?

I wasn't. I did not stop and think about what I was doing. I couldn't resist staying away. On her birthday. I had to be there. Seeing her inches away from me, smelling her, watching her dance... How was I supposed to keep my distance? How was I supposed to wait?

I knew the rules well, and what I did was cheating, but I didn't care. That parasite worked with her. He was given a head start. I had to do something. I had to make her see me first. I only thought if I did, she'd feel me, like me, bond with me so that she would choose me when the time came.

But it was a mistake. I hurt her, put her in danger, and now she wouldn't even look me in the eye. I let my lust and love for her overtake me. I fucking bit her for moon's sake.

What if it was more than a love bite? What if I had really bitten her?

"Hey," Kayden nodded at the coffeehouse across the street, "I found her."

Stopping in my tracks, I jerked my head toward the glass walls where she sat behind. Her forehead rested on her hand as she stared vacantly at the table. Then her finger wiped under her eyes. Was she crying?

My heart hurt with all the pain I'd caused her. She'd seen enough. It'd killed me she had to be out there alone all this time with that motherfucker without any interference from us. It was her path that would lead her here to the pack. To me.

Now, instead of making it up to her, wiping away all that shit she'd seen, I'd made her more miserable.

She was probably afraid I'd tell someone about what we did last night. The student who would brag about tapping the teacher, stupidly exposing her. The rumors that might cost her the job and the reputation she'd just gotten back. But the only danger I posed to her was the beast that had once…

"Come this way before she sees us." Kayden dragged me from where I stood and my pitiful monologue, and then we hid behind a few trees in the park across the coffeehouse.

"Now what?" he asked.

"I'd go talk to her, but she wouldn't listen to me." I yanked my gaze from her and peered at him. "She might listen to you, though."

He glared at me, snorting. "You want me to clean up your mess?"

"Aren't you Alpha?"

"Yes, which means I kick your ass for what you did, not clean up your fucking mess."

"C'mon, Bro…"

He crossed his arms over his chest and let out a low growl. My ass of a twin was stubborn as fuck. I knew that look on his face by heart. It meant he wouldn't change his mind willingly.

My shoulder lifted in resignation as I backed away from the trees. "Fine. Then I'll go tell her everything. It's the only way she will—"

He gripped my shirt, his hand too strong on the back of my neck, and set me back where I'd been. "Are you out of your mind?"

I shrugged him off me. "I don't know what else to do. All I know is that I need her to understand. I won't let that parasite win her over. I just can't."

He shook his head, his jaw twisting, eyes distant as if he was deliberating what I'd said with himself. "We've got to ease her through it, not dump it all on her head like that." The shaking of his head grew faster. "No, Alec. She'd hate you even more."

"Then go talk to her before that fucker steals her away!"

He was about to protest again, but a certain foul stench choked me and made him look like he was about to hurl his guts out.

"Speak of the bloodsucker." He prowled out of the park. "Keep him busy while I go talk some sense into our Belle."

CHAPTER 12
KAYDEN

A few groups of people were milling around, waiting for their coffee orders, and the noise coming from inside the coffeehouse is a discord of conversations, clattering cups, dishes and country music. I easily picked Belle's sniveling voice in the chaos. "...Katrina, I fucked up. I really need your help, but I hate to ask you to drive all the way back. So if you haven't left Forest Grove already, please come over. I'm at this...Red Moon Café, a few blocks from campus."

It wasn't hard to guess who she was talking to on the phone. I took several deep breaths to calm down the fury roiling inside. First it was the bloodsucker's stench, now hearing Belle asking for help from the…

My head went blank when she lifted her eyes from the table and landed on me. The way her big eyes bulged made me fear for her health. Seriously, she had enormous hazel eyes; she'd make a cute lemur.

"What are you doing here?" she whispered between her teeth, her gaze wandering right and left. "Isn't it enough what you've done already?"

I raised my hands up in surrender. "Uh…wrong twin. Kayden, not Alec. I come in peace."

She looked like she was about to cry again. "That's…"

"A little creepy that you can't tell us apart?" I rolled my eyes as I grabbed a chair and sat at her table. "I know, right? Tell me about it." Then I took off my jacket, showing her my full sleeve. "To make it easy for you, I have this, while Alec only has a tiny tattoo on his left shoulder."

Here came the lemur eyes again. "You can't sit here. I can't be seen with you." She shook her head. "Either of you."

I rested my arms on the table and leaned forward. "I'm sorry, Professor, for the nuisance my brother must be causing you right now, but we really need to talk. Do you have a book?"

She scowled. "What?"

"I'm your student. You're my teacher. If you worry so much what people will think when they see us together outside school, this conversation will look more than normal to them if we have a book on the table."

She blew out a long sigh. The she bent to get her bag on the chair next to hers. Some…cleavage went on display. Even though I had full visual before, knew exactly what these beautiful tits looked like and would love to see them again and again, I was surprised my first instinct was not to look but to find out if anyone else was looking. And gouge their eyes if they were.

Fundamentals of Abnormal Psychology textbook replaced the view and landed between us on the table. She opened it then buried her nose in. "Fine, you want to talk? Why don't you start with why neither of you were surprised to see I'm your professor?"

That was a tough one to answer without revealing the whole deal. I should lie. I must lie.

Why was it so fucking hard to lie to her?

I was taking forever to answer. She must have noticed because she lifted her nose a little and fixed me with a death glare. "He knew who I was when he…"

Here we go. "You're a national celebrity. The whole country followed your case. Everybody knows who you are, Belle. It's—"

"Professor Ferro to you," she hissed. "And even if you knew about the case, how did you know I was teaching at your university?"

"Your name is listed on the course."

"No. They haven't had the time to change it yet. Only Professor Asher's name is listed for that course. I checked it myself."

Fuck. Time for some reverse psychology. "Professor, you've done nothing wrong. You're both adults. You weren't his teacher last night. You're making a big deal out of this for no reason."

If I thought that glare she was giving me earlier was her death glare, I was wrong. This one was. "No reason?"

"I'm sorry. That came out wrong." *Tactically.* It stopped her from asking about how we knew her. "With the case and just getting your job back, I understand what is at stake here for you."

"No, you don't. How could you understand? You're just a boy whose brother tapped the teacher's ass."

What she said was legit, but it did hurt. I fought so hard not to tell her the whole truth so she would understand and put us all out of our misery. But it would only bring up a bigger misery, especially on her.

"Do you know how my ex-monster got me fired from the university?" she continued. "Without my consent, he had taken a video of me while I masturbated for his pleasure, under his commands, in his office. Then he coerced a student to fabricate the video to make it look like I was masturbating for said student."

Disgust flipped my stomach. "What?"

"He gave the video to the faculty. They forced me to resign, and as a courtesy to Professor Montgomery, they kept it confidential provided that I'd never teach anywhere else."

I should pay that fucker a visit at whatever dump he was at and punch a hole in his face. "I'm so sorry you had to go through this shit."

"You want to know what's really at stake here, Mr. Beastly? If your brother told anybody I was involved with him, the whole country that followed my case would turn on me in a heartbeat. Instead of being a victim of power abuse, I'd become the whore who slept with her teacher for good grades and professional gain, and fooled around with her students behind the poor guy's back, then falsely put in him in jail so she could screw her own students." She kept her voice low all the time, looking around to make sure no one was in a hearing range.

"But—"

"It wouldn't matter if I didn't know Alec was my student at the time or that I wasn't his teacher when it happened. And all the horrors Professor Montgomery did to me would be portrayed as fabricated lies by the whore. Not only would I lose my job…again…but also the monster that made my life a horrific tragedy could walk freely."

Sadly, this was the world humans lived in. In my world, which soon would be her world, things were settled differently. I couldn't wait for the day when Belle was finally one of us so I would put an end to that fucker who hurt her once and for all.

I meant…so Alec would end him.

My gaze traveled to where I knew my brother was hiding. These feelings sneaking up on me, this overprotectiveness for Belle growing inside me with every moment I spent looking into her eyes…were treacherous.

"Alec will never hurt you, never let you be hurt."

She snorted. "What's that supposed to mean?"

She didn't know it yet, but once she chose a mate from our pack, he would be her protector and everything she needed. It was how we were wired. Swoon head over heels with our mates, unable to see anyone or anything else. Possessed and obsessed with them. A blessing and a curse all in one.

"It means exactly that. He won't hurt you." My gaze returned to her as if I couldn't stay away for another second. "Neither will I…Professor."

"Even if I believe you're good people who wouldn't hurt their professor like that, should I convince myself neither of you would get drunk at a party, blurt it all out, brag around?"

"You have my word," I promised. "No one will ever know. I'll help cover it up, too, so you can still be together."

Her jaw fell. "What are you… It was a one-time thing. Will never happen again."

"You know as well as I do that is not what's going to happen. He likes you." *Loves you to bits.* "And I believe you like him, too. There's no reason in my book why the two of you can't be happy."

"No." She blinked and swallowed. Her gaze dropped to the open pages. "It doesn't matter if I liked him. It's wrong. Taboo," she whispered, and jealousy stabbed me hard. "Besides, he lied to me. About not knowing me, about his age—"

"One day you will know why he had to, and these standards will no longer matter."

Something flicked in her eyes when she looked back at me. "What does that even mean?"

The vampire's stench filled my nostrils, suffocating me. *Damn it, Alec. You couldn't hold him back a few more minutes?*

"Oh my god." She hid her face with one hand. "Please, don't see me."

Anger pulsed through me. "You shouldn't be afraid of that…Asher. Not when I'm here."

She didn't seem to be listening. Her hand moved away from her face, and she stole a glance up. "Oh my god. He's just walked in. Kayden, please leave. If he sees me with you, I'll get into so much trouble."

"Professor Ferro!" The bloodsucker's filthy voice penetrated my back.

I held my breath, my fists clenched so hard my knuckles went white. Then I tilted my body to the side, spreading my legs to the tiny aisle, hoping he would trip over my feet.

He threw me an obnoxious smirk as he glided away from my trap, then he lifted Belle's bag and helped himself to the chair. What a dick!

"Kayden." He glanced at the open book. "So eager to learn on your very first day. I'm impressed."

I blocked my nose as long as I could. "It's hard to pass the opportunity when one finally gets a decent teacher."

His ugly mouth twisted with a full smile, fangs and all. I wanted to pluck them out of his jaw.

Belle, who was sitting as a ghost, pale and silent, since the blood sucker set foot in the place, cleared her throat. "You know each other?"

"We go way back," Asher said grimly. "The Beastly twins have been my students from day one."

"I see." She grimaced. "Anyway, I was just explaining a few things and telling Mr. Beastly that he needs to refer to you from now regarding any further explanation." She looked at me, her face stern. "I will no longer be teaching your class."

"What?" *She can't just push us away while this*

bloodsucker has her all to himself. "No."

"It's for the best."

"You can't do that," I snarled, the beast threatening everything.

"Kayden," Asher grumbled a warning.

Her chest heaved as she glared at me. "Excuse me?"

Shit. I can't lose control like this. Not here. "I'm sorry. I mean…we, your students, will be devastated to see you go."

She snapped the book closed and stood. "Thank you, but it was just one class. Regardless of how much we both enjoyed it, no one gets that attached to their teacher when they've only taught them once."

"True. You sound so creepy sometimes, Kayden." The fucker smirked again.

"I can't agree more," she said.

Are you shitting me? I needed to get out of here before I destroyed everything. Literally. "Fuck you," I mouthed at him without her seeing me as I got to my feet.

"Can I please have my bag, Professor?" She extended her hand toward him.

He was hugging it on his lap like a sick stalker. How could she think I was the creep here? "Of course." He handed it to her as if he did absolutely nothing out of the ordinary.

"Thank you." She shoved the book back in

the bag. "Now if you'll excuse me, I'm a bit tired and need to go home."

"How about I give you a ride, Professor?" I asked.

Her brows hooked, her eyes alarmed. I really needed to tone down this protective shit a notch or two. "Thanks. I have my own car."

Asher left his seat. "Then allow me to drive."

I'm going to kill this pretentious bastard.

"No." She stared at both of us in disbelief. "I don't know what's happening here, and I hope it's just an Oregon thing for all the men to be so…" Her fingers clawed and retracted in the air. "I don't know what it is, but I'd like you, both of you, to take a step back." She left the table, practically jogging away out of the place.

The moment she left, I channeled all my rage at the vampire. "What the fuck is wrong with you? You just have to ruin everything, you bloodsucking shit?" I was boiling, yet I kept my voice low. A habit when talking about anything involving fur or fangs.

His lips curled up in a low snarl. "Everything is already ruined because of you. What the fuck were you doing sticking your stinky dicks in her? And the bite? This is not the deal, Beastly. If you're not going to play fair, I won't either."

Damn it, Alec. I hated the position he'd put me in. What my brother did was wrong. Cheating, like the asshole just said. And now I had to stand here, get lectured for it by a fucking vampire.

"The bite is merely a graze. A human could have left a deeper one." She would be transitioning by now or, at least, her smell would have changed if it had been a shifter bite.

I pushed my chair away, leaving the table. Then I held my breath as I gripped his shoulder. "Back off, Asher. Belle is Alec's fated mate."

"That was never true." His disgusting breath and voice fell too close on my ear. "And something tells me…you want to believe I'm right."

A chill ran through me. Did he notice? If he did, Alec might have noticed, too.

Fuck this shit. He was playing dirty mind games like vamps always did. I glared at him, contemplating clawing up and ripping his throat apart. That would be quite a mess to clean up, though. He wasn't even worth it.

"I see the way you look at her, Kayden. But save your breath." He pushed my hand off him. "Rena has always been mine."

"Not this time, leech." I shoved him out of the way and stormed back to Alec.

His heavy brows hitched. "I know you're mad, but I couldn't hold him off any longer."

"It's okay." This wasn't the reason my blood was simmering. It wasn't the bloodsucker either.

I was mad at myself.

The feelings I had for Rena…Belle were wrong. It was happening so fast, invading me like an unpredicted storm. I couldn't allow myself to fall for my brother's mate. That would ruin us and the pack.

"Did it work?" he asked. "I saw her leaving, and she was pretty upset."

"Don't worry, Brother. She will come around," I mumbled, a lump in my throat. "I won't let anyone come between the two of you." I held both his arms and looked him straight in the eye. "Anyone."

Not even me.

CHAPTER 13
BELLE

I drove aimlessly for hours, trying to wrap my mind around the day's events. Then it fucking rained—poured—and I had no idea where to go. Katrina had gone AWOL. I didn't have a single person to talk to or seek help from. Even my therapy started in two weeks in Portland; I didn't want to spill my heart out to a therapist that currently worked at the university, and that was the earliest appointment I could find in Portland.

At times like these, I missed my mom more

than the norm. The one who raised me, not the one who dumped me as a baby. I'd never met my real parents, and I knew so little about them. They were Italians. Some said they died in an accident. Some said they just took off. The bottom line was that they had disappeared, and I was left alone.

I never wanted to dig around and find what really happened. Sometimes, the truth was the worst. Besides, Mom was enough for me. She took me in when I was three. It was just the two of us in a cozy home that was always clean with plenty of food.

She was a great mother and a great high school French teacher. She used to live in the French Quarter in New Orleans. Then she moved to California to be a teacher. That was how I met Katrina. She was a student of Mom's and visited a lot to be tutored…and when things got rough at home.

I didn't remember much of what was going on with her family, but I remembered her father used to beat her. Then one day she became the rebel she'd always been and exploded in his face in the middle of our street. I was too young to remember what she'd said, but the man never laid a hand on her or anyone else after that night. In fact, he'd never spoken again either.

Then Mom died when I was eighteen, and everything went south. If it wasn't for the college scholarship, I wouldn't know how I'd have wound up.

Still, I'd married a man twenty years older than I was, who beat the hell out of me and almost killed me, but marrying Declan was a normal outcome for someone like me.

I didn't want to be the bitch who analyzed herself to make up pathetic excuses, because I wasn't. Suffice to have said, I had serious abandonment issues and daddy issues to say the least. These alone would cause anyone to make some serious mistakes, like falling for the first daddy figure I'd met or staying in an abusive relationship afraid of being alone.

But it could have been worse. At least, I had my degree to fall back on.

My job was the only thing that mattered now. I had to protect it no matter what.

My stomach growled. I hadn't eaten anything but that sandwich at lunch. If I went home, I wouldn't bring myself to cook anything once I saw the bed. I wanted this day to end in any way, and sleep was the best escape.

Miles from home, I turned on the GPS and drove to the next restaurant. Stopping the car under the Grizzly Grill sign, I eyed the horde of motorcycles parked outside. I hoped this place wasn't one of those biker's hangouts.

I hurried inside, sheltering my hair with my bag, making another note to self to keep an umbrella at all times in the car because this was fucking Oregon.

The restaurant was more like a diner with a little bar and a pool table, quaint, small and relatively clean. Certainly not a regular biker's bar or club or whatever they called it. It was packed with all sorts of locals. Still, I felt out of place with my suit and bag, especially when the leather-clad, big men crammed around the pool table stopped gulping their beers and stared at me.

Pressing my thumbnail, I found myself an empty booth as far as possible from them and scooted in.

The waitress gave me a menu. I was too hungry to look. "Can you please just get me the fastest edible thing you have here?"

"That hungry, huh?" She chewed on her gum, writing down what she decided to be my order.

"And in a hurry."

She glanced at the bikers over her shoulder then back at me. "They might look scary, but they're harmless, sweetie. Not the ones you should be scared of around here."

She ambled away and yelled my order at the kitchen. I didn't bother to ask her what she meant or even think about it. I just wanted to stuff my mouth in peace and go home.

I ran a tired hand over my neck, massaging it a bit until I hit a sore spot. The mark Alec had left. Quickly, I removed my hand and let my hair cascade down, as if someone would see.

Nobody cares about you or your love bite. Nobody even knows you here.

My eyes swiped the place, confirming my thoughts. No one was looking at me. No one recognized who I was.

Why did everybody keep saying they knew me from the case then?

The waitress returned with my food. A burger, slice of pie and a beer. "Enjoy, sweetie."

My eyes narrowed at her. "Hey, do you know who I am?"

Her lips puckered as she shrugged. "Should I?"

If a couple of college senior boys and a male professor did, then a local woman, who worked at a gossip pit, definitely would. "Have you ever heard about the Beauty and the Beast case?"

She blew a bubble with her gum. "No,

sweetie, sorry."

I gave her a quick smile. "No worries. Thank you for the food."

My mind swirled with suspicions. Alec pursued me on my birthday. It wasn't a random hookup. And after my conversation with Kayden, I was positive something out of the ordinary was happening with the twin.

Joshua, too.

The three of them possessed qualities and bodies that made smart women go stupid. I was no exception. Alec with a dick that fucked like a beast. Joshua with his mesmerizing looks, voice and charms. Kayden with his protective alpha bravado, and the *I like you but can't have you* act I picked up today and actually believed.

I was stupidly crushing on each of them, enjoying the attention, shutting down my brain. How desperate was I for that kind of care the three were showing me even though it was fake and most likely hiding behind a dangerous motive?

How much trouble would I get myself in for one passionate night or—

"We've got to stop meeting like this."

I squeezed my eyes shut, my heart thrashing, dread and anger roiling together inside me. "You've got to be kidding me." My eyes flicked up toward the voice that managed to set a throb in my pussy every time I heard it. "Are you following me?"

Joshua laughed quietly, already sitting. "I'm starting to think it's you who are following me."

I cocked a brow, having a serious urge to throw mustard on his sexy, smoldering, all black clothes, and then take them off, mash my burger against his face and chest, and eat it off him, licking his body clean.

Wait a minute… NO! That was not what I was going with, brain! Work with me here!

"I'm not joking. Are you stalking me, Professor?" I asked.

He stared at me with his breathtaking eyes. Then he frowned. "Of course not."

"Then why do I keep bumping into you everywhere I go?"

He shrugged nonchalantly. "You just happen to be at the best eating places in town. Looks like someone has already been showing you around, and you don't need my help in that department."

"Nope. I just stumble upon them."

"You're so lucky."

"Lucky?" I couldn't. I just couldn't. "Please get another table. I'd like to be alone."

He wasn't moving for a few moments, not

even breathing, just staring. Then he nodded once. "As you wish."

As he left the booth, I sighed in relief. Then I jumped when he crouched down by my side. "What the hell?"

"You are a smart, beautiful woman and a talented teacher. You should be making others walk on eggshells around you, not the other way around. You have so much power, Isabella. It's all in there. You just have to find a way to pull it forth."

Did he just say my name, my whole first name, with that voice? Did he just say I was beautiful?

Dizzy, I just looked at him. I was not ready for this. Should I respond? Walk away? If I stood up, I was pretty sure I'd fall over.

I knew what I should do. Shoot myself for being irrevocably stupid to want to hear more of his words when I perfectly knew he was just distracting me from seeking the truth.

I loved the way he was talking about me, and it was working. It started to sink in that I might have been paranoid for no reason, and all I needed with some confidence in myself rather than doubting no one would care or like me without ulterior motive.

His gaze entered mine, taking a piece of me with him. I wanted to go. I wanted to follow him wherever he was going.

"Is that all I get? A blank stare?"

I blinked. "Yes."

His eyes dipped to my mouth, and he licked his lip. "I have to tell you that I find you very attractive. You are virtually irresistible to me, and it has nothing to do with whom you remind me of."

"Wow."

He stole another glance at my lips. "Wow?"

I shook my head, swallowing. "I mean, why do you have to tell me that?"

Rising to his feet, he smirked. "For when you find your power and decide you can date another teacher again."

CHAPTER 14
JOSHUA

I retreated to the shadows, to the darkest spot of the restaurant where she couldn't see me anymore. I watched as she munched on her burger, loving every gesture. She ate like a beast. I couldn't wait to feast with her. I bet she would drink a body dry before I got a chance to taste it.

Oh how much I wanted to taste *her*. If she knew how much I loved her, how I'd protect her, how I'd do everything in my might to make her happy, she'd just give herself to me right now and never look back.

This time, she was mine. The twin animals would have nothing on the hell I'd planned to unleash upon them if they thought of touching her again.

Fated mate my ass. They would say anything to have her.

Every creature wanted a piece of you, my beloved. Even the devil himself.

But you're mine, Isabella. Don't ever forget that.

I'll protect you from them all. Even that pathetic human coming on to you now.

She disdained the drunken jerk, slowly chewing her food, her nose crinkling with disgust.

He wouldn't take a hint, of course. Good. I was hungry and ready for dinner.

He leaned in, his filthy breaths on her forehead. "Why are you being so stubborn? You like to play hard to get?"

She dropped the rest of her burger on the plate. "You need to leave right now. I told you I'm not interested."

"You and I are going to happen. The sooner you get that through your thick skull, the better off you'll be."

Oh no, you didn't.

One of the bikers scorned the asshole, telling him to respect the woman's wishes. Yet again he wouldn't listen.

In a blur, I reached Isabella's table. By the look on her face, I could tell she was astonished and relieved to see me. "Is there a problem, here?"

"This doesn't concern you," he said.

Standing a few inches taller than him, I stepped in, turning his body toward me. "The lady doesn't want to talk with you. You should go."

"Lady?" he snorted. "Why don't you get your ass out of here and go get your own bitch?" He grabbed Isabella's arm. "This one is mine."

When she yelped and her heartbeat thumped in my ears, my composure went down the gutter. I gripped the bastard's hand and twisted his arm behind his back. Taking the back of his neck in a tight grip, I banged his head on the free table next to Isabella's. I didn't want to splatter blood on her food.

He groaned a few swears, fully incapacitated. I was sure I broke a bone of his in the way, too. "When a lady tells you to leave, you fucking leave." I glanced at Isabella over my shoulder. "Get in your car and lock it. I'll be right there in a second."

CHAPTER 15
Belle

I locked the car the second I was in it, but that wasn't enough to make me feel safe. An unwanted hand on me triggered a shitload of dark memories to resurface. My breaths raced, my pulse drummed, and I thought I was about to have a panic attack.

I rummaged through the backseat, looking for anything to breathe in. Then a knock on the window almost stopped my heart. I whipped my head toward the sound to see it was only Joshua.

With my chest heaving and fingers shaking, I opened the window.

"Get in the passenger's seat, I'm driving you home." He took one look at me then his jaws hardened. "That's not a request."

I moved as he asked—ordered—without arguing. I didn't want to. I loved that he was here, doing all this.

As I settled in the other seat, I unlocked the car. He got in quickly, something crumbling in his hand. Then I realized it was a to-go bag. "Your leftover," he said.

He beat the crap out of a guy and then had them pack the rest of my meal? I would have laughed but I was having trouble breathing.

"You don't look so well," he said. "You look like you're—"

I yanked the paper bag out of his hand, pulling the containers out frantically.

"—hungry."

Glaring at him, I buried half of my face in the empty bag. I was hungry, though. I'd been all day— PMS? It was the least of my concerns at the moment. Breathing came on top of feeding.

His eyes widened. "Or you're having a panic attack. Fuck. Okay, just keep breathing. Deep breaths. Do you have any panic disorders? Nod."

I shook my head.

"Okay. Good." His palm fell ice cold on my back as he rubbed it, yet I welcomed it. He breathed with me, deep breath in, deep breath out. His other hand found my arm, and he leaned closer to my body.

I wished I could have snuggled into his arms and buried my lips inside his mouth, not in this recycled bag.

"It's not going away. Do you have any Xanax or Valium?"

I shook my head again, dizzy, quivering, my eyes tearing up.

"It's okay, Isabella. You're going to be just fine." He enveloped me with his arms and pressed me close to his chest.

Wow. I'd never wished for something, and then it'd come true this fast. Or turned out to be this good. Closing my eyes, I found a better breathing speed, anxiety instantly slimming.

"I'm here," he said. "I wish I could take it all away, the pain, the fears. I wish I could show you the world is not as terrible as you believe it to be now. There are dark, evil things out there. But they are such a small part of the world there is no reason to be in constant fear. Not anymore. I'm here."

His words soothed me better than any

drug. What was going on here? Where was all this coming from? He was just telling me what I needed to hear, but it felt so real, so intense. This couldn't be an act. No one was that good.

My head lifted, and I looked into his eyes as they connected with mine. There was something out of this world about them. It was easy to lose myself there, never to be found.

As my breath evened, I needed the bag no more. All I needed was the second half of my wish to come true.

He stared at my lips for a moment that seemed to never end, causing my heart to leap in anticipation, then at my neck, right where the love bite was.

Self-conscious, I swallowed, but I didn't try to hide it the mark. I wanted this kiss too much to care.

His lips parted as he lifted his eyes to mine. "The panic attack is gone. I should get you home."

Just like that, he pulled away and started the car.

CHAPTER 16

BELLE

Only the sound of our hearts accompanied us up to my apartment—or was it only my heart?

When I was pressed to his chest, I didn't remember hearing his beat accelerating or feeling his skin warming or anything a man who liked a woman should have felt.

Surely, as he let the perfect moment for our first kiss go by, he confirmed he didn't like me like that.

Didn't he say I was beautiful, *virtually*

irresistible, and he wanted us to date? Or was it all my imagination? And if he didn't want to kiss me, why did he insist on taking me up to my apartment?

Perhaps he was asexual or religious. Perhaps he was being a gentleman, and I was just a horny slut.

I unlocked the door and stepped inside, but he wouldn't. He just stood there, holding my leftover and my bag.

A smile tugged at my lips. "Are you coming?"

He grimaced, his face so pale in the dark. "You need to invite me in."

"Seriously?" It was impossible not to laugh. "Are you a vampire or something?"

His body stiffened and his grimace hardened.

I grabbed my things from his hand. "That was a joke. You need to lighten up a bit."

"You still have to say it if you want me to come in."

"Fine." I placed the stuff on the console table under the mirror and turned on the lights. "Please, come in, Professor Asher."

"Thank you." He carefully set one foot inside, then the next. "Please, call me Joshua."

"All right, Joshua. Would you like some tea?"

His lips stretched with a smile. "I'd love that."

I entered the kitchen, his footsteps following me. The place was small enough for me to listen to his breaths as he watched me. It made me nervous and excited at the same time. Biting my lip, I wondered if he was checking me out, how he felt if he was…

Get over yourself, Belle. Charming or not, he's a creep who has been stalking you all day. Don't forget that.

A creep you've just invited in your place, dummy.

My brain kept screaming at me, yet I was numb to all the danger Joshua entailed. My body welcomed and enjoyed it, already dying for his touch.

Just like with Alec.

Last night at the club was a demonstration and an urge to take the control over my life I'd long lost by doing something extreme. And now, my attraction was also an attempt to take control. To change today's horrible narrative into something appealing.

The more dangerous the better.

Because even if I got hurt, it would be my doing. I took a chance, and it went south. I wasn't forced into it. It was all my choice.

"Thank you for what you did at the restaurant," I said without looking at him.

"It was nothing. Happy to do it every day."

My hands tightened around the kettle. "Are you going to tell me why you've been following me since I left the campus?"

Silence fell too loud on my ears as I felt him close the distance between us. Frozen in place, I waited for whatever he was about to do. Speak, touch me, grab a knife…

But nothing happened.

"Joshua?"

"I already told you," he whispered. Then cold fingertips ran along the sides of my neck.

I gasped, a shiver running through me. "So you have been following me?"

His long fingers—the first time I noticed how exceptionally long they were— snaked around the front my neck, and his chin rested on my shoulder. "Yes."

I sucked in a hissing breath, terrified now. I was no stranger to fear. The one Joshua induced in me was a different kind than Declan's. This one I'd started to crave, not abhor.

And it made me wet. So wet.

Why I knew Joshua wouldn't hurt me, why I wanted him to take me here and do whatever he wished with me was beyond my intelligence. But I liked every moment of it.

I needed it.

"Why were you following me?" I repeated.

"I feel very protective of you, Isabella."

"That's a line from Twilight."

Suddenly, he backed away from me, leaving a terrible emptiness around my space. Why did I always say the first thing that came to my head that I never intended for the public?

"The one where vampires sparkled?" he mocked.

I rolled my eyes, turning to face him now that I'd ruined our moment. "Yes."

"Well, I never watched that." He leaned against the counter. "But I'm intrigued to know. Were you Team Edward or Team Jacob?"

Finally making that tea, I chuckled, and then returned my gaze to him. "Neither. I'm a why choose girl."

His eyes narrowed at me with genuine interest. "A why choose girl?"

"It's when the girl doesn't have to choose and ends up with all the guys."

"That's…greedy."

"Oh c'mon. If you could have more than one woman with them okay with it, would you choose?"

"I would." The answer came unhesitant and authentic. He didn't have to think about it for one second. He just knew. "I'm a one woman man."

The kettle whistled, and I poured the tea in two black mugs. "Those are rare to find, not even in romance books. Sugar?"

"No, thanks."

"Me neither. I'm going to have that pie with it instead." I walked to get it. When I spun to return to the kitchen, I bumped into his body. A gasp escaped me as our fronts collided, and I felt him, his need poking my stomach, his gaze raking me from head to toe.

He didn't touch me, but he didn't move either. He just wanted me to know how he felt for me with physical proof. I wished I could have done the same. Taken his hand and showed him what he was doing to me. Instead I just shoved the paper bag between us. "Share it with me?"

A wince contorted his face, and his teeth clenched. He looked like he was about to snatch the food and throw it away then pounce on me.

Yes, please.

I never made the first move. I didn't know how. He had to do it. Get over whatever he was struggling with and do it. *DO IT!*

But he stepped back. Again. "Anything you want, Isabella."

Really? That was it? Damn it, Joshua. Why

do you have to be such a Jane Austen guy? Didn't he know as much as a girl wanted pie, she wanted cock more?

I stalked into the kitchen, got the damn thing out of the bag and grabbed two plates and a knife.

"Why did you decide to leave the class you were so eager to teach?" he asked.

Changing the subject completely now? Fine. "You were right about stressing myself out. I should take it slow," I lied. Then I proceeded to cut his slice.

A little bit too harsh.

"Shit!" I jerked my finger, blood streaming down.

Before I stuck it in my mouth, Joshua reached out quickly and grabbed my hand. He held my finger in front of his face, gazing at it as if hypnotized.

Then he looked up at me, his beautiful gaze glowing, smoldering, holding mine. And he stuck my finger in his mouth. His tongue slid over my wound, warm and wet licking at my finger, sucking on it—all of it.

I moaned. Hard. He wasn't sucking blood off my finger. He was sucking my phantom dick, and I was about to come.

He pulled my finger out. It seemed to be much better, no longer bleeding, the wound only a tiny scrape.

Had he actually sucked the blood off the wound?

I imagined what other good uses I could put that mouth to....

"Too gross for you?" he asked.

Gross? Was that what he got from the moans and the look on my face?

Note to self: you really really need to work on your horny face.

This could be gross to some, but for me it was sinfully delicious. Even romantic. We had exchanged an intimate moment. The two of us had connected far beyond what was considered appropriate given our professional relationship to each other.

At this moment, I didn't care about anything, how the world would see me if I jumped into bed with another professor, on the very first day of my new job. I wanted him to touch me in every possible way, to push his body against mine and make sweet love to me.

How could he not see that?

"No. I find it very sexy," I blurted out, my chest rising and falling with every shuddered breath. In romance books, men noticed and appreciated that view. Did he?

"A man touched your arm and you had a panic attack. Is that how you're going to react if I kiss you? That's the only reason stopping me from doing just that."

"Oh." *Oh.* Everything made so much sense now. He wasn't asexual or religious. He wasn't an asshole. He wasn't a creep. He wasn't anything but a panty-melting hotness with the manners of an eighteenth-century man.

And I liked it. Loved it. All of it.

Joshua was a loner like me. With PTSD like me. The only difference was that he knew how to live with that, saw the world the way it should be seen, had the confidence to move on to the best of his ability.

I envied that about him. I wanted to reach that, too. And I believed from the moment I'd laid eyes on him, he would get me there.

My arms moved on their own accord, wrapping around his neck. My body leaned into him, my heaving chest now pressed against his as hard as I could. I let my hips thrust forward to see if that erection was still there.

Holy fuck. He was twice as hard.

I couldn't wait any longer for feeling it inside of me. I licked my lip, bending his head to me. "How about we conduct an experiment to find out… Professor?"

CHAPTER 17
JOSHUA

Her mouth parted, and I could taste her sweet breath as I licked my lips and took hers between mine. Oh, that felt so good. The soft warmth of her mouth against mine, the life behind it, her energy, the smell of her blood, all of it was so enticing that I could hardly think about anything but my need for this one woman.

Rena.

In all her reincarnations.

I had a feeling this one would be the last. No more waiting. No more fighting the filthy beasts over the love of my life.

Oh, Isabella. How much I wanted your soul to live forever. With me.

Her mouth opened up a little more, caressing my lips with her own. Our mouths intertwined as our tongues writhed rhythmically against each other. She moaned softly, her breasts pushing against me, beckoning me to touch them.

It was pure lust for her. She didn't have the time to feel anything else for me, while I…

Two hundred and fifty years, Isabella. I'd fallen for you two hundred and fifty years ago.

Had she known how many times I'd waited for her to come back only to have her for a few years before she'd die again, she would have felt me, felt safe with me, known how much she meant to me.

And hopefully, loved me.

She paused for breath, her eyes half-opened with arousal as they met mine. "See? I didn't have a panic attack. It's just my heart that's about to stop from that kiss."

I took a deep breath, the smell of her wetness filling my nostrils, sending a nagging pulse in my cock. "I understand you just need to feel pleasure, have a good time to erase this heavy day. And I'm more than delighted to provide that for you. The truth is I need this probably more than you do. But before I take this any further, I want you to know, whatever you're thinking or suspecting, I would never hurt you, Isabella. I would do anything I possibly could to keep you safe and happy."

Not waiting for a reply, I kissed her harder, my cock aching to be freed. I could not wait to be inside her again, feel her tightness around me, make good love to her and show her how much she meant to me.

Now that the time had arrived, I couldn't stand the anticipation any longer. I pushed her jacket off her shoulders, careful not to rip it off. Then I pulled her blouse up over her head and threw it to the side.

I savored the sight of her breasts in that bra before I undid it and let them hang bare in front of me.

She gasped. "Can you turn off the lights?"

Perplexed for a second of the sudden request, I almost snorted. Why would any woman that beautiful ask not to be seen? Then I saw it.

The scars. On her abdomen, chest and arms. Some were faded, some barely healed.

She sheltered her body with her arms. "Please?"

"No." I held her tense body so hard before she'd think my pause had anything to do with her body. It was my rage that I was attempting to control, the bloody images of my needed vengeance over that piece of shit that hurt the woman I loved. If I lost it now, I'd lose her, too. I just couldn't let that happen, not after she was finally in my arms.

"You're beautiful. Perfect just the way you are." I looked at her so she could see I meant every word. "You don't ever have to hide anything from me. Do you hear me?"

She eased in my embrace. I savored her lips one more time, unable to keep my hands to myself. I filled one hand with her breast, stoking it slowly, rotating my thumb over her nipple, carefully observing how it was affecting her. Her moans of passion grew, and her hands were tugging at my t-shirt. I shrugged off my jacket and slipped the t-shirt over my head for her.

"Wow." Her fingertips glided up my abdomen, feeling the contours of the muscles and reaching my chest, tracing my tattoo.

The talsam that allowed me to walk in the sun. Courtesy of the devil himself when I and the shifters had made the deal with him. The agreement that brought Rena back to life. I got to not turn into ash under the sun, and they got to shift on demand.

"You got a very nice...tattoo." The softness

of her touch was too much to bear. I moaned quietly, my need for her mounting painfully.

"You're so hot, Professor," she murmured.

The way she said *Professor* drove me crazy every time. I wanted to take this slow, but she was making it impossible. With a hiss, I yanked her up in my arms, her breasts bouncing in my face. Then I placed her on the counter, lifting up her skirt in the same move.

A quivering gasp escaped her, but then she smiled. "So strong, too."

My hands slid up the sides of her thighs. "And you are so extremely sexy...and naughty...Professor."

She bit her lip, the smell of her arousal more intense. "You like it when I call you that?"

"I do." I ripped off her panties swiftly, and she gasped again. I spread her legs with my hand, the other wet with her juices from drenched lace. "So much."

My gaze fell between her thighs, at the trickling trail her desire for me had left. Between that and the panties in my hand, I didn't know how much willpower I had left. I needed my cock inside her pussy and my teeth in her veins.

A groan ripped from my throat, and I went on my knees, burying my face inside her. A delicious shiver engulfed me as my tongue took that first taste. It wasn't any different from Rena's. Same old sweetness that blurred my sanity and turned me into a hungry predator.

My mind and body began to surrender to the pleasure. I pushed my tongue into her slit, into the wetness and slurped the mind blowing nectar. She gushed heavier, and I was at the mercy of her immaculate scent. I inhaled sharply, over and over again, growing harder as I smelled and ate her pussy, lapping the juices into my mouth.

I found her clit, licked it carefully not to let my teeth touch it. It protruded against my tongue. Her hands plunged into my hair now, and she purred and hissed and moaned.

I licked harder, faster at the sensitive nub with gossamer pressure. Her body undulated up and down, riding my face. My hand gripped her ass, the other fondling her breast, kneading it while I fucked her with my tongue.

My cock ached, my balls engorged, begging for release. *Please, come now so I can thrust my cock and every lament need I've had for you inside your heaven. The only heaven I would ever go to.*

I entered her deeper, and she clasped around my tongue, her fingers ripping at my hair, her screams a frenzy of yeses and happy curses.

I sucked every drop, fantasizing I was drinking her blood instead, not that I wasn't enjoying these scalding hot juices. They were so good they unleashed all my deep, forbidden desires for her, unshackling my self-imposed restraints.

Rising to my feet, I started to unbuckle my belt, hoping when I let out that one need, the other would blur away. But her fingers worked the buckle faster and pulled my pants and boxers down to my knees, the brazen gesture making me even thirstier. My cock swung free while my mouth watered. I needed to taste her blood as much as I needed to have her.

Her eyes widened. "You're really blessed in that department."

A woman saying I had a big cock was always flattering, but I wasn't really listening. I was fighting so hard not to make the worst mistake of my life.

I closed my eyes for a second, reminding myself of what was at stake here. If I bit her now, she'd never be mine again. My thirst silenced my mind in a heartbeat. My control almost nonexistent, I peered up at her neck, at the two throbbing veins calling for me to do the one thing I needed the most.

The ugly bite glared at me, provoking me even more to replace it with mine. It was clearer, now that the makeup faded away, and it looked worse than I thought. But what if the shifter bite had already consumed her? Kayden assured me she wasn't transitioning, but the mark had never faded.

If either I or they turned her before she'd made the choice, we both would lose her for good. I—

"Are you okay?" she asked.

My teeth clenched as I dragged my gaze away from her neck. Then I lifted her roughly off the counter and swiveled her so that her back faced me. Her ass was the perfect distraction. I rolled her skirt up to her waist, and I bit at each cheek—I had to bite something.

"Ouch," she moaned.

"I'm sorry." I kissed the sore flesh, wiping my thumb around it to soothe it a little. "Did that hurt?"

She tilted her head to look at me, her hair sliding off her shoulder revealing that fucking mark again. "Yes. But I like it." She swallowed. "Pain is all I've known for ten years. I've learned to enjoy it. Even ask for it."

I didn't need to hear that. It was disturbing

and arousing at the same time, and I was already out of my mind. Pushing her down, I spread her ass as far as possible without tearing her up and slid the tip of my cock into her wet pussy.

Her body squeezed against mine until I was all the way inside of her. She let out a muffled scream as she braced against the counter, bending lower and spreading her legs farther.

"Fuck," I groaned as her positioning allowed for even more penetration. I held her long hair and wrapped it around my fist. Then I pulled it as I found my rhythm in and out of her.

Her hips bucked into mine, rocking against me. "Oh, Professor. You feel so good. So fucking good."

I slammed harder into her scorching tightness, utensils falling off the counter with loud clinks. With a spank on her beautiful ass, I pulled her head up by the hair, her long neck exposed. I thought fucking her would cool my thirst down, but I couldn't have been more mistaken.

The disgusting bite flashed, and my inner beast hit the surface. I tilted my head back, swiping my tongue over my teeth.

"Oh my god, Joshua. I'm coming again."

Hearing her screams of pleasure and feeling

her tightening around me were all I needed to explode and for the predator to burst free.

I opened my mouth widely, and with sharp fangs, I speared the fucking shifter's mark.

CHAPTER 18
ALEC

A fucking mess.

I was unable to concentrate, obsessively thinking about the smell of her panties. They were burning a hole in my bedroom nightstand for a week while I sat here, in the woods at dawn, at a bonfire pack meeting.

It had veered off-topic again, and I'd tried my best to look like I gave a fuck what anyone was going on about, but as soon as the endless debate of bears were more badass than wolves came back up, I was done.

All I could think about was her anyway.

Fuck. That body. That smell. That skin. I would've licked her from toe to neck and back again if she'd given me the chance.

"Hey." One of the bear twins handed me the circulating bourbon bottle. "Where did you go?"

I lifted the bottle to my lips and immediately regretted it. How could a drink I'd had every day since puberty suddenly remind me of one of the best lays of my entire life?

As if I'd forgotten.

I couldn't take my mind off Belle. Especially with that parasite hovering around her day and night. "I'm killed by boredom. I am sitting here, quite dead with the rivalry talk. Aren't we here to figure out what we're doing about Belle?"

"Easy, Alec. It's the same old doubleganger shit we deal with every fifty years," he said, and the second brother laughed.

I clenched my teeth. "Rena has never been a doubleganger. She dies and gets reincarnated."

"Whatever you howl, Wolf. The bottom line is, you and the leech are fighting over that voodoo reincarnated girl for the hundredth time. What else is new?"

"What's new is that he's winning," I seethed and jumped to my feet, leaves crunching under, bourbon spilling down. Belle had shunned Kayden and me, wouldn't even talk to either of us. And Asher's smell had been all over her all week.

"The wolves and the bears aren't exactly best buddies, but the last time I checked we're still brothers. We all belong to the same pack," I said. "Do you really want to see that parasite living off an innocent human? Sucking her blood? Turning her? You know damn well Asher can't be trusted. Vamps have no control."

I knew the bears never liked that deal we made with the devil two hundred fifty years ago, but they still hated the vamps.

The bear brothers exchanged glances. "I didn't see you getting all worked up about human lives when you shook hands with the devil himself."

"Guys, bringing this up again won't solve any problems." Kayden joined the conversation abruptly. He'd been silent, only observing, from the beginning of the meeting.

"Maybe, but it seems that your brother needs the reminder," the bear brother said, looking at me. "That deal you made put us at a fucking peace with the vampires. We can't touch our natural enemies. They get to live and hunt, and we just watch. Have you thought about how many lives Asher has taken so your precious Rena gets fucking reincarnated? Lives we were supposed to save from him? Or Rena's is the only human life you care about?"

I scratched the back of my head and peered at Kayden for support. He just looked away.

Seriously?

It was no secret my own twin blamed me, too, for what I had to do to save what was left of my mate. But he'd never done it in front of others.

It hurt. I didn't need this from him right now neither did I need the reminder from the bears. I blamed myself every day for the consequences. Having to live with the vampires on the same land, with equal hunting rights. Turning a blind eye to their kills, only to wait every fifty years for Rena to make a choice.

To join the pack or go with the vamp.

They thought that didn't hurt me enough every fucking day, every fucking second?

Whoever won got to spend the rest of her allowed years on earth as her mate, and the other had to leave Forest Grove until…her time ended.

Then we would start all over again.

Live with the enemy. Wait. Fight over her. Wait again for Halloween night when she would make her choice. Live the next few years accordingly. Repeat.

A sad loop Asher and I had agreed to revolve in because we had no choice but to do just that.

I couldn't just let her die and never come back. I couldn't face an eternity without her in it. Waiting to have a few years with her every fifty years was far better than living forever without seeing her again.

Yes, I'd doomed my pack with me, and there wasn't a day when I didn't wish there had been a way where I was the only one that suffered.

But I had to save her.

It wasn't all about my selfish love for her and my refusal to just let her go. It was about her.

Rena came from a cursed bloodline. Hadn't I made that deal that night, her soul would have gone straight to the devil. I couldn't just let him have her. I had to do something, and that was the only deal the devil agreed to make.

"An interesting game I would like to

watch," he'd said.

The rules were clear.

No shifter killing vamp. No vamp killing shifter—as if they could.

No interference from either Asher or I in Rena's life before she willingly came to Forest grove.

No turning her before she chose a mate.

She had to make her choice by Halloween night.

No immortality for her. Upon her choice, her mate could turn her, yet Rena would still die every time she was fifty to be reborn.

On the devil's side, he wouldn't screw her as long as we followed the rules or else he would lose his claim on her.

Breaking any of these rules broke the deal, and the devil would claim her soul, forever making her his.

A disgusting deal made for the entertainment of the devil and the suffering of our species. But it gave me Rena back.

I had no regrets.

My eyes swiped through the accusing faces around me. Then I nodded. "Fine. Blame me all you want, but before you do, remember we all got something out of that deal, Bear. No more Full Moon shifting. The control over when and where you change… Yeah, it looks like it's you that need the reminder, not me." I took off my shirt and twisted, ready for a run. "I'll figure out what to do with Belle on my own. Thank you for the help, *Brothers*."

"Alec..." Kayden's voice died in the sounds of my morphing bones.

I shifted into the beast I'd always been, digging my claws in the dirt. Then I raced the cool wind deep into the woods.

"Alec, wait!" The shouts died behind me. I didn't listen. I had one thought on my mind.

Go to Belle and make her mine. Whatever it took.

CHAPTER 19

ALEC

I wore the beast out with the run. Then fed it a whole deer before I morphed back into my human form. The morning sun sparkled gently on the trees, warming the air as I reached Belle's block.

In the thick forest, I could see she was already up from the bay windows of her apartment. She walked around in a thin gown that wasn't doing much to cover her underwear or nipples in that light. Instantly, my cock hardened. The memory of me inside her played on repeat in my head.

She didn't seem to notice me or know I was even there. Like every day I lurked here, watching out for her, making sure that prick wouldn't harm her.

Today would be different.

I would make her see me. In every way.

She was alone, holding a cup in her hand, smoke trailing out of it. Coffee. The fresh aroma had spilled here. Asher wasn't there like he'd been for four days and nights in the past week.

Perfect.

Pushing the heavy branches, I emerged from behind the trees. My eyes glanced up at her as she mused at the sunrise. The street was so quiet I could tune away everything else and listen to her heartbeat. I wished she could hear mine, too.

Her lips touched the rim of the cup and froze in place as her gaze collided with mine. Her big eyes widened, and I smiled, lifting a waving hand.

Her mouth hung open, the cup fell from her hands, and her eyes grew even wider.

She looked terrified. Did I creep her out again? I thought I had a nice smile. It was certainly prettier than the parasite's. What the fuck did she see in that—

I was knocked off my feet and landed on my ass with a figure blacked out by the sun on top of me. It took me a second to identify its smell. Belle's.

What the fuck? How did she get here so fast?

She placed her index finger on her mouth, her long hair draping around us. I could barely see her face, but I figured she wanted me to be quiet. I wasn't complaining she was straddling me right now, but what the hell was going on?

Another familiar scent filled the air, and instincts pulsed.

I looked to the side, into another two sets of eyes, big brown ones, surrounded by fur, lots of fur.

Yeah, the bears were here.

Swiftly, I pushed her off me and bounced to my feet, ready to fight. Whatever they were here for, they should have come in their human form. They knew better than to be around any human as beasts. It wasn't safe.

"No, Alec. Stay down," she whispered.

Was she scared for me? Did she actually run down here to…rescue me?

I liked the sound of that. Loved it.

"It's okay. Just go inside and lock the door," I whispered back, glancing down at her curled body on the grass.

She shook her head vigorously, her face white as snow, and then she pointed at me and herself. I presumed she wanted us both to sprint for the apartment building.

Of course, she didn't know I could take the twin bears in a flash. All I cared about was her safety. I really needed her to get out of here. If they were here to stop me from talking to her—I wouldn't listen—it could get…messy.

Deep growls burst from the grizzlies. One of them lifted a paw, and Belle's heart rocketed. I pounced fast, taking one down, yet he clawed my arm as I did.

It seared as I jumped up, the other bear getting closer. When I was about to lunge at him, hands dragged my shirt with enough force and speed to yank me out of the woods and into the building.

The door slammed shut. I stood in the dark stairwell, Belle staring at me with her enormous eyes.

"Are you out of your mind? Who the hell attacks a *bear*? Your blood is all over the place, Alec!"

I checked my arm. It was hardly any blood. But to her, maybe it seemed like a lot. "I'm fine. How did you get down so fast? And how, for the love of the moon, you dragged me like that?"

"I don't know. Adrenaline." She threw her hands in the air in exasperation. "I was so scared. You're such an idiot." Her eyes roamed my arm. "And you're not fine. Come with me."

She started up the stairs, and I was more than happy to follow. Finally, I had a legit excuse to be in her apartment without her worrying about what people would say. Finally, I would have a chance to talk to her, maybe even…

A devious smile crossed my lips. She was so sexy in that sheer gown I could tear it up and take her on these very steps or against the wall. Again.

She let me in her place. I had to duck a little as I walked around afraid I'd break anything. I was too big for this miniature of an apartment. "Cozy," I said.

Her eyes narrowed at me as she pointed at a couch. "Sit down."

I did, and she disappeared into a room I assumed to be the bathroom. When she came out, she had a robe covering her body and a first aid kit in her hands.

I mourned the lost view in silence. She set the kit on the cherry wood coffee table and went away again.

"Where are you going?" I asked, the pain in my arm more real now. I healed best in my wolf form and could stand the pain a lot better.

"Getting something sterile to clean the wound." Her voice came a little distant, more of an echo.

She returned with towels, a big set of bandages and a basin of hot water. She put everything on the table and sat next to me. The heat emanating from her soothed my pain. Her very existence next to me, this close, had always done wonders. For a beast fated to a mate like me, her presence alone was enough for life to be good again. I couldn't help the smile on my face.

Carefully, she put a towel on my thigh right under my wounded arm, and dipped another towel in the water. "Why are you smiling?"

"I'm happy."

"You were almost attacked by a bear. Then you threw yourself at it. Now, you have deep gashes, oozing with blood, covering your arm. You probably have bruises all over your body, too, and you're happy?"

"If all that didn't happen, I wouldn't be here now, knowing that you cared enough to save and help me, watching that beautiful expression, feeling your touch again even if it is tending my wounds."

She bent a thumb under the rest of her fingers and ran a hand through her hair. "Anyone in my place would have done the same."

"No. They would have called the cops or animal control, and then bolted their doors, not flown down to the rescue."

A long sigh seeped out of her mouth as she pressed the wet towel on the blood. "You need to take off your shirt."

My brows shot up in disbelief. "Really?"

"Not for…" she grumbled, "I must check if you have other wounds or bruises."

"Oh." I lifted a hand to the upper button, a little embarrassed. As I moved down to the last button, I caught her peeking. I smiled again, shrugging off one arm, looking into her eyes. "Should I take off my jeans, too? It will give you a better view."

She looked away, lifting the wet towel, a shy smile twitching on her lips. I tried to shrug the second arm and moaned quietly. Her hand reached my shoulder and finished the job for me.

"Thank you, Belle."

She tore her gaze away from my half naked body and cleared her throat. "Professor Ferro to you."

"No." I tucked her hair behind her ear. "We're not at school, so I'll call you by your sweet name."

She sighed again and pushed my back forward gently. Her touch set a tingling through my whole body. "Bruising is already forming around your shoulders. Maybe we should go to a hospital to check if anything is broken."

"No hospital. I have everything I need right here."

"Alec…"

"Nothing is broken, Belle. Not bones anyway."

She shook her head and pressed the wet towel to my arm a little too roughly. "What were you doing here, Alec?"

I growled in pain. "I came to talk to you."

"I already explained to your brother—"

"My brother hasn't tasted you, hasn't felt you shake around his cock, hasn't had one of the best moments of his life inside of you."

Something flicked in her eyes, a mixture of anger, embarrassment and arousal. She took my good hand and put it on the towel. Then she got up. "Keep the pressure here. The bleeding isn't stopping."

"Where are you going again?"

"Coffee."

"Do you have any bourbon instead?"

She came back with a…bag of coffee. I scratched my head. "What are you doing with that?"

The couch sank beside me as she sat. Then she exposed my wound, took a handful of ground coffee and covered my wound with it. She repeated the process until the gashes were all buried under a mountain of brown powder.

"Is that…sanitary?" I asked.

"Yes. It will stop your bleeding so I can stitch you up."

"Thanks, but I don't need stitches. I'm a fast healer." I gazed at her, impressed. "But how did you know all that? That was not covered in the medical training course."

A terrible darkness loomed over her for a second. Then she shrugged. "How do you think?"

The muscles around my heart squeezed. It had taken all my restraint, all my patience, not to go and save her from that fucker back then. But I had to stay away, mind my own fucking business, until she came here on her own.

The devil had always put Rena through shit, provoking me to break our deal. I would have, many times before, if it wasn't for Kayden and the pack. They'd always stopped me in time. Despite everything, they were happy for me every time I got to be with my mate. Came to think of it, this might be what they were here for today.

To create an opportunity, to help me win her over.

I chuckled.

"What's funny?" she asked, working out the bandages and the sewing kit.

"Not what you had to go through, of course. But how things could turn out to be in the end."

Her gaze pierced me. "You sound much older than your age."

"I told you I was old. You didn't believe me."

"Your school ID begs to differ."

I rolled my eyes. "You can't deny it's hot to date a younger man as much as I can't deny it's hot to date an older woman."

"Not when that older woman is your teacher."

"That makes it even hotter," I whispered, a chill running through my spine.

She swallowed. "We're not dating, Alec. We just…"

"Fucked against a wall? Seriously?" I leaned forward, my mouth a few inches from hers, the urge to silence her with a kiss unbearable. "Look me in the eye and tell me it was just sex and you feel absolutely nothing for me?"

She huffed and fiddled with the med kit. "I'll bandage you up, and you can get the stitches at the hospital. I'm running late for class."

Without thinking, I grabbed her wrist, blaming her with my eyes. How could she not remember how she felt for me?

"Let go of me," she said.

I took one more glance at those lips, and I just couldn't stop myself. "Never." I crushed my mouth against hers. She resisted at first, then her lips and tongue moved invitingly.

Closing my eyes, I groaned, my cock a solid rock. She tasted so fucking good, so vulnerable like this. But I wanted more than a taste or the hard fucking I hoped would follow that kiss.

I did the best I could to pour down every emotion I'd had for her in that kiss. Suddenly, she pulled away, as if she'd just realized what we were doing. Her fingers flew to her mouth, and she winced.

"Belle, I lo—I love everything about you. I swear to you it's not just sex to me. You blew my fucking mind."

"Alec, I can't," she pleaded.

Frustration burned more than my arm. "Tell me that kiss didn't do something to your heart, not just your pussy, and I'll get out of here and never bother you again."

CHAPTER 20
BELLE

I couldn't say it.
I couldn't lie.
I'd been convincing myself it was just sex, but it wasn't. No matter how many times I'd denied it, even been scared to admit it to myself, I was attracted to Alec, and not only physically.

There was this...thing I couldn't explain that kept dragging me to him. Something old. Ancient. As if our souls had met before, in a different life, at a different time.

And it felt so terribly right.

Were we destined to each other in a past life, Alec? I never believed in soul mates or any of that new age reincarnation and spirituality—a debate I'd always had with my colleagues. But this...all this with Alec...and Joshua, even Kayden, felt so familiar and pleasing.

But how?

Even if it was true, how could I confess my feelings to him? How could I let myself get carried away without risking my entire future and perhaps even my life?

I stared back into his smoldering eyes, the golden strikes that gleamed with his need, and fought against the urge to take off those jeans and ride him hard on my sofa bed. Ugh, even my furniture wanted me to drown in taboo sin.

My sex drive was another story. It was killing me. Since my birthday, I'd been horny twenty-four seven. This very boy, sitting before me, seducing me to do more nasty things to him, had unleashed a beast that night. Add that to the fact that I hadn't had any action since the time I was with Joshua...

I fanned myself, begging brain to win this battle over pussy.

It lost.

Again.

I had serious self-destruction issues. I really needed my therapy. Thank goodness for embarrassment, though. That lady had saved my ass from taking that huge cock of my own student all inside me.

Why was I embarrassed? Well, the last time I had sex, I blacked out.

I was really enjoying myself with Joshua, and the last thing I remembered I was fucking coming for crying out loud. Then everything went black. I woke up in my bed, alone, covered in sweat, cursing myself to hell and beyond.

Why would I blackout during amazeballs sex?

Who does that?

Even though Joshua visited a few times after, hoping he'd have taken it from where we'd left off, I couldn't embarrass myself again.

And if losing my job to another scandal that could set a monster free wasn't enough to stop me from thinking about riding Alec's cock, my humiliation for blacking out during sex was.

"You can't say it because you'll be lying to yourself before me." He winced. "You feel something for me, too. Something strong.

Maybe so strong you're afraid. But I'll protect you, Belle. From everything."

"Could you please stop talking?" Every word, every whisper when he was this close, in need of my care, half naked, his taste still on my lips, was clouding my mind, numbing my rationality, driving me toward a path that would never end well. "You're worse than the devil."

His body stiffened, and he seemed to be...offended? "You don't know what you're talking about. It's the devil that I'm trying to protect you from."

"What?"

He glowered and rested his back on the sofa bed. "Nothing."

I wasn't going to drop it this easily. I'd been ignoring all the weird things happening in this town for my own sanity. But every day it only got crazier. Something was going on between the twins and Joshua. I knew it from day one. The feeling that it had something to do with me wasn't an illusion. I had to get to the bottom of it. "Are you referring to Professor Asher?"

He rolled his eyes, his jaws tight.

I grunted. "So you only speak when you're trying to get into my pants?"

He flounced like an angry trout, coffee

powder falling off his arm and thankfully on the towel, not on the sofa bed. "I came here to talk to you. I wasn't just saying things to get you into bed." He held my gaze, his hand on my arm, rubbing it gently. "I want more. Much more. I want all of you, Belle."

Damn. He was good at diversion. I was about to get lost in his eyes and melt with his lips again, letting go of what I wanted to know. A senior beating me at my own game?

Sorry, not anymore.

I, too, touched his arm. Holy fuck, he was made of rocks. My palm slid up to his shoulder and onto his chest. His heart skittered under my touch, and so did mine.

Not the best tactic, Belle.

It might be working on him; I could feel him dropping his guards, his body not tense anymore. But it was doing the same to me.

And when he held the back of my neck and whispered my name into my ear, his cheek to my cheek, I was giddy, my lashes fluttering, my pussy clenching.

Focus. Don't look into his eyes. Or at his lips. Or at the bulge growing bigger in his jeans. Fuck. Stop enjoying touching these unbelievable muscles and speak.

I gulped. "Does your feud with Professor Asher have anything to do with the woman he couldn't protect?"

He froze. Even his heart skipped a beat.

I'd suspected it since that day at the coffeehouse with Kayden and Joshua. Now, Alec's body gave me the answer I sought.

"What woman?" he asked, his voice hoarse.

"The one who has my face."

He drew back, the golden strikes aflame. "Asher told you about Rena?"

And now I had a name to the mystery woman.

"You both loved her," I speculated. "Then something bad happened…to her?"

"What did he tell you, Belle?" His fists clenched, and his face turned crimson.

Even though I knew better, his anger didn't scare me. It only pushed me to go further. "You think he hurt her, and now you're trying to protect me from him, maybe even from the same destiny she had to suffer?"

And Joshua was hoping for a second chance with me to correct whatever he had done.

Alec shook, his chest rising and falling with heaviness he kept unrevealed. "What did he tell you?" he whispered.

"Not much. But I hope you will."

He closed his eyes. "He didn't tell you anything, did he? I should have known when you touched me you were playing me." A bitter chuckle burst out of him. "Well played, Professor."

I started wiping off the coffee, evading his gaze. As I cleaned it all up, no more blood was coming out of the gashes. In fact, the wounds turned out to be a lot less deep than they had seemed. "Look at that. You might not need stitches after all."

"I told you I'm a fast healer."

I made sure all the openings are clean and bandaged half of his forearm. "You're good to go."

He gave me one last gaze, and then he put on his bloody shirt and got to his feet. "Thank you, Professor."

Was it so wrong that I wanted to give him a hug? Even drive him to college on my way? I wanted to prolong our time together now that he was cutting it short so abruptly.

What was wrong with me?

"Do you need a ride?" I regretted the offer the second it fell out of my mouth.

"It's best if we're not seen together in public." His voice dripped with blame and mockery. "I can see myself out." The back of his head and his perfect ass said his goodbyes.

He opened the door and stepped outside. Then he twisted and leaned on the doorframe with a piercing look. "One day, you will know everything, and you will be smart enough to know that when you have to choose between us, you'll choose me."

CHAPTER 21

BELLE

I thought the department meeting was going fine, but when Pattison asked to have a word with me alone after, I became nervous.

"How are you doing, Isabella?" he asked.

Isabella? That's new.

I smoothed my skirt and shifted in my seat. "I'm doing…great. Thank you for asking, Professor."

"Please, when we're alone, feel free to call me Damien." He left the chair behind his desk and came to sit in front of me.

I pressed my thumbnail hard. I didn't like whatever was happening here.

He smirked at my hand. "An anchoring technique?"

"Yes." I smiled anxiously. "Wow. I didn't know anyone noticed."

"I like to be thorough and might notice things others seem to neglect, for professional purposes. They say the devil is in the detail."

"I prefer the original saying."

"Which is?"

"God is in the detail."

His face tensed, and a red glare flickered in his eyes that vanished the second I blinked. Falsely spooked, I frowned. It must have been my imagination.

"Speaking of things I've noticed that may not be clear to others yet," he said, "you and Joshua?"

Oh. So this is what the meeting is about.

"What about Professor Asher and I?" I played dumb, hoping across all hope this was all about Joshua and not a certain huge Beastly twin.

"You're dating."

"Not exactly. We bumped into each other once at a restaurant and—"

"Things evolved," he interrupted, and

irritation pulsed in my veins. I hated to be interrupted even if it was by my boss. "These details I do not need to know." He leaned forward. "All I'm saying here is that if you are going to date, you should report it to HR so you won't get into trouble. It's protocol."

I nodded. "Thanks for letting me know."

A devilish smirk curved the corner of his mouth in the scariest yet most alluring way. "But if you decide to date someone like…let's say, Alec Beastly…"

My heart tumbled in my chest and sank to my knees. I pressed my thumbnail so fiercely I thought I broke a knuckle. "Why would I date Alec Beastly?"

"Why wouldn't you? Why would anybody remake a mistake?"

I felt that my heart was about to explode. How the fuck did my boss know I fucked Alec the night before I worked here? Did Alec tell him? Was he upset about this morning that he exposed us? How fucking naive was I to think Alec would keep our secret like he'd promised?

Or was it Kayden who did it? Or someone else entirely, someone who saw us that night?

What was I going to do now?

"Professor Pattison, I…I…" I stammered, tears pricking my eyes.

"Relax, Isabella." His index finger touched my knee. For attention? "I'm not trying to make you uncomfortable. You don't know how much I like you. How much you mean to me."

Is he coming on to me? Is he blackmailing me, thinking I'd spread my legs for him to avoid the scandal? "No, I don't. Why would I mean anything to you?"

He leaned back. "Because of Katrina. She's a very dear friend, and she asked me to look after you. This is me looking after you."

I swam in a whirlpool of confusion and mixed emotions. I didn't know what to think anymore. Was Damien making a pass at me or did he just like Katrina? Perhaps too much?

Why the hell did a jealousy blade stab me? Where was this coming from? Damien was a very attractive man, a silver fox without the silver, a blond fox. He had the body of a twenty-year-old, the wisdom of an intellectual and the prestige of a college professor. Yet not once had I felt attracted to him.

Why now? When he practically posed a threat to me?

This side of me that kept shoving me into dangerous situations since I came here and got a kick out of it, when did I get it?

Professor Pattison rose and moved behind

my seat. "Sometimes mistakes happen. Some other times, we like these mistakes so much we make them again and again." His hands tightened around the back of my chair. "Because wrong is the only thing that makes us happy," he whispered in my ear. "It's not fair to stay unhappy all the time, is it?"

"No. It's not," I murmured as if hypnotized, my breathing shallow.

"A few mistakes wouldn't hurt, Isabella." His breaths tickled my ears, relaxing my senses, sending a strong throb between my legs. "Someone like you should be cut some slack. Someone like you deserves to be happy."

"Someone like me?"

"An amazing person who has suffered much more than any of the snobs who made the rules standing between people's happiness."

His words seeped into my pores like a drug. I looked at him over my shoulder, his face more attractive up close. I'd never taken notice of the shape of his lips. Staring at them longer than usual was painful. I felt as if I was going to come just by looking at them, imagining the taste and texture and strength of their kisses.

"You want me to be happy, Damien?"

Who was that woman speaking now? That was not what I called my boss. That was not my voice. I'd never speak that seductively or assertively not even to a stripper dancing on my lap.

"More than anything," he murmured.

Dazed, I felt as if I was having an out of body experience, watching from afar my life turning into one of my favorite reverse harem books ever.

I'd fucked my co-teacher, my student and now I wanted to bend over for my boss.

Yeah, that will make me happy.

Oh, note to self: add Kayden to the harem. I'll be sandwiched between the twins while Joshua and Damien take care of my holes.

My big, wet pussy agreed with a double clench.

Second note to self: keep a pair of fresh panties in your bag if your pussy is incapable of staying dry around any man in this damned school.

"A beautiful woman like you should feel nothing but happiness." Damien's breaths danced on my lips, getting too close to mine. "So take what's yours, Isabella. No one needs to know. No one."

The next thing I knew, our tongues were twirling together, and his hand was in my bra. The kiss tasted like sin concentrate. The perfect way he cupped my breast made me wet like I'd never been before.

He knew exactly how I wanted to be touched, how I wanted to be kissed, as though he'd been watching me my whole life, learning, taking notes, preparing for the moment when he would have his hands on me.

His free fingers dipped to my waist and found their way beneath my skirt. He slipped beneath the soaked lace of my panties and slid a finger over my clit, dipping down into my hot juices.

My heart pounded with a mixture of excitement and anxiety. "We're in your office," I said against his mouth, and then our tongues met again.

"I'm aware."

"Anyone could come in and see us," I reminded myself between kisses.

He entered me with his middle finger, then added another. He moved his thumb in small circles, but kept his fingers pressed deep, unmoving. "And you're getting wetter by the second because of it."

Once again, I was letting my pussy take my reason away, hide it in this dark corner where I couldn't find it.

This was wrong on all levels, and my clit

was already so protruded and engorged I felt I was going to come any second. I liked wrong. Loved it. Got off on it. And this man, Damien Pattison, who moved his fingers as if he knew where every nerve and fold of my pussy were by heart, was a force of energy. I was unable to pull out of his orbit.

I couldn't fathom how, in the span of a few minutes, I was afraid he would expose or fire me, and now I was letting him finger fuck me in his office and was fucking happy about it.

I stared at his arm, his dress shirt peeking out from his suit jacket, and could feel him watching every single breath I took, every gasp and every time I bit my lip to keep from making a sound.

His knowing touch built a heavy ache in my belly, and I pushed into him, wanting more.

Footsteps echoed behind the closed door, but Damien moaning my name eclipsed the sound. I moved my head to the side, watching the shadows of people passing by the office behind the tainted glass.

"Look at you," Damien said, leaning to kiss my neck just below my ear. His breath was warm on my skin, and I was torn between focusing on his touch and fretting about the people walking right outside. The combination of his touch and the fear of being caught almost made me fall to pieces.

As if he knew this, Damien murmured, "No one out there knows you're about to come all over my hand."

He pressed his thumb hard into my clit. I bit the inside of my cheek to keep from crying out. "That's it," he whispered, rocking his palm against me as he slipped a third finger inside. With this, he stretched me to the blissful edge of pain.

He watched me fall apart at the indecency, the thrill of doing something irrevocably filthy. "Oh, fuck, Isabella. That's it."

My nails dug into the leather cushion below me, and he pumped his fingers in me, his shoulders rocking. My head fell back against him, letting out loud moans matching the pleasure he'd had unleashed in me, unbothered by who might hear me.

I groaned as he prolonged the orgasm with his fingers pushing even deeper. He slowed, and stilled, before kissing my temple, and then pulled his fingers out. Lifting his hand from under my skirt, he pressed his fingers to his mouth, and then he licked them, watching me. "Your tongue tastes like candy, but your pussy tastes way better." He leaned in and kissed me deeply. "I want it to be my cock inside you next time."

Yes, please.

Jesus, who was this woman possessing my brain? I wanted his cock, too. Even after what he'd just given me, I wanted to climb onto his lap and take all of him inside. "Oh God."

His face stiffened all of a sudden. I blinked, and he was no longer standing behind me, licking my cum. He was sitting before me, staring at me with that red glare again.

My eyes widened. "What the hell?"

A small smile eased his expression. "Are you all right, Professor? I think you broke your nail. Your finger is bleeding."

My stare examined my thump, confirming what he'd just said. My head whipped up at him. "How did you get to this chair so fast? You were standing right behind me."

He shook his head in confusion. "I was sitting here all the time, Professor. I was talking to you about colleague dating protocol, and you zoned out," he pointed to my hand, "and broke your nail."

What sick game was that? "No. You were standing behind me, and you were…"

"I was what?"

Did I imagine all that? Not possible. The scalding gushes hadn't even cooled yet.

He was looking at me like I was a crazy person now. A case to analyze. Oh my God.

What if I blacked out again, had a wet dream in front of my boss…that featured my boss?

No. No! It felt so real, so good to be a dream. Or was that too good to be true? "When you blackout, you do not dream. Something is wrong. Is this a trick?"

"Isabella, you don't seem so well. Why don't you go treat that nail and take the rest of the day off?" He was already on his feet, gesturing at the door. "Do you need me to show you where the infirmary is?"

"No. I can find it on my own." I barely had the strength to stand without fainting. "Thank you, Professor."

A devilish smirk found his lips. "Any time."

CHAPTER 22

BELLE

I need to have sex.

I'd been denied real pleasure for years, only used to please a sick monster. Then this portal of hot, satisfying sex opened, and my body and mentality craved it so much they behaved sickly in its absence.

Add what had happened with Alec this morning to the equation, and I got a huge conflict between what I wanted to do and what I shouldn't be doing, one I'd been suppressing for days. My subconscious was under too much pressure and needed a release.

The day dream.

What I'd experienced was a typical ID-Superego clash that resulted in a day dream not a blackout.

Cold water ran down my thumb in the staff bathroom as I psychoanalyzed what had happened between Damien and me. The dry blood under my nail was hard to remove. Maybe I should have let Joshua suck it.

I laughed at myself and headed back to my office—Joshua's office we shared.

"Are you all right?" he asked the second I entered, his deep wince already on his face.

"Yeah." I nodded reluctantly as I sat at my desk.

He took off his glasses and came over to me. "What happened with Pattison?" His eyes landed on my hand. "And your thumb?"

"It's nothing. The nail broke in the middle. Worst case scenario, they will remove it, and it will grow back."

He glared at me. "What disturbed you so much that you had to press your nail hard enough to break it like that?

"What? How did you know I did that?" Fuck me. First Damien and now him. "Don't tell me you noticed, too?"

"You do it all the time. It's hard not to notice," he said quickly. "What happened, Isabella?"

Should I tell him? Confide in him until I finally went to therapy? I did need to tell someone, and I felt Joshua could be the one person I told such things.

"Did he touch you?" he asked under his breath.

The way he asked took me by surprise more than the question itself. "What? Why would you say that?"

"Just answer me." He banged the desk surface with his fist. "Did he touch you?"

"No! I...I don't think so."

"What do you mean you don't think so? It's either he touched you or not."

"I don't know, Joshua. One minute he was... The next he was sitting in front of me, his hands far away." I shrugged, staring back at him, agitated. "I had a fucking day dream. That's it."

A dark flick I'd seen before struck his steel gaze. "About him?"

"Yes," I whispered inaudibly.

"Fuck." He was fuming.

"What is this all about?" This couldn't be jealousy. We only hooked up once. I never mentioned anything about dating him, exclusively or otherwise. "Why was Damien touching me the first thing you assumed?"

"Damien?" he scoffed. "Do you need me to drive you to the hospital?"

"No. I can take care of myself. Now, answer me. Did he do it before? To someone you know?"

He spun and headed to the door. "I have to go."

"To Rena?" I dared.

He stopped short and his heels raced back to me. "How did you know that name?"

Fuck, piss and shit. That backfired fast. To explain, I had to tell him about Alec. *Well done, Belle.*

I twisted my lips and glowered at the floor. "Answer my questions first."

"You want to know everything? Fine. Come with me."

CHAPTER 23
KAYDEN

Alec paced from one tree to another like a caged wolf. His rambling didn't make any sense. Belle, that little thing, had supposedly flown out of her place at lightning speed and had enough strength to drag this bull into her building with the same speed.

"This can't be. I think the bear claws are messing with your head with their venom," I said. "You need me to suck that out for you?"

"You're not listening! The fucker bit her!"

he howled, his eyes glowing with the beast's golden flames. "She's turning."

"The bloodsucker is a lot of things, stupid ain't one of them. He would never deliver her to the devil on a silver plate like that. He couldn't have turned her, Alec."

"I saw the marks on her neck!" His clothes ripped off him as he half-shifted, claws, fangs and wolf hair on.

"You sure they were the vamp's? I mean, you bit her, too. It could be your old bite or he did just the same. A love bite." My phone chimed in my pocket. I got it out and saw it was Asher calling.

In all honesty, I thought Alec was exaggerating, having another *the parasite stole her from me* moment, but Bloodsucker Fucker blinking on the screen on the same day got me worried.

"Asher is calling." I glanced up at my brother, who dashed at me, and took the call. "Kayden."

"We have to meet. Beast Clearing. I'll be there in thirty minutes. Belle is coming with me," Asher said.

I took a deep breath, watching Alec consumed by anger, fully shifting now. "We're already there."

Hanging up, I rubbed my twin's wolf head.

"Asher is bringing your girl here, and we'll figure this out. Looks like you're going to tell her everything you wanted to this morning and couldn't after all."

CHAPTER 24
KAYDEN

An engine died right before the hiking trail. Must have been Asher parking his car at the nearest spot to here. It wasn't easy to find this place through the woods. The clearing of the willow tree, also known as Beast Clearing. As it was famous for being a place where big wolves and bears liked to chill, very few were eager to explore the area or go off their hiking trails to find Beast Clearing.

Where we hung out, held our pack

meetings, let out steam, and where the devil's deal had been made right under the willow tree.

Leaves and twigs rattled. One heartbeat raced in my direction, the smell of fear tagging along. Lots of it.

On the other side of the woods, Alec's beast heart was rumbling. I'd told him to go for a run and vent so he would come back in his human form when she arrived.

And I remained in the middle. Waiting. Being the Alpha.

What was the charm about this position? Why would an entire pack fight for it? From where I stood, it had zero glamour, only burden after burden.

The Alpha couldn't go after what they wanted. They went after what was best for the pack and its members. The Alpha couldn't behave the way they wanted. Couldn't feel the way they wanted. Control the anger. Control the fear. Control the desire.

Control the heart.

A gust of wind spiraled from the right. I turned, and Belle was on Asher's back, arriving in a blur.

He put her down and held her staggering body. "Where's Alec?"

"Running," I uttered.

"How the hell did you do that?" Belle asked in a whisper, dazed.

I rolled my eyes at the leech. "Did you bother to explain anything before you went all Twilight on her?"

"I didn't have time." He kept rubbing her arms, and I pictured ripping his off his shoulders.

"Explain what?" She was sobbing now, her eyes darting between us, then examining my shirtless body. "Why are you half-naked…in the woods?" Her stare flicked at Asher. "Why did you bring me here? This is abduction." She nodded frantically. "Yes. This is what abduction looks like."

It took me a moment to realize what this must have looked to her. "Oh, no no no! Belle, no one here is going to hurt you. I…I was swimming at the creek. Alec will finish running, take a dip and come here, too, so we can talk. *Only* talk."

"Then fucking talk!" she yelled and twisted at Asher. "How could you run this fast?"

He waved a hand aimlessly, his mouth parting for a second as if trying to find the right words, and then he just shrugged. "I'm a vampire."

She scrunched her nose like she'd smelled a fart. "Seriously, Joshua? Is this your idea of a joke after this day I've been through?"

"He's not joking, Belle," I said.

"Yeah, and you're a werewolf. Ha ha. Very funny. The next thing you'll tell me I'm that Rena woman's doubleganger," she mocked. "Yeah, I've seen all the movies, watched all the shows and read all the books."

"Reincarnation," I mumbled.

A scowl ruined her beautiful face. "Excuse me?"

"You're a reincarnation, not a doubleganger," I explained. "Rena gets reborn every fifty years. You're the same person, not a double."

"Ah…okay. Whatever you say, *Wolf.*" She made a face and glared at Asher. "I don't know what the FUCK is wrong with you," her glare shifted to me, "or you, but thanks for the entertainment, boys." She backed away and spun, heading out of the clearing. "By the way, vampires don't wear glasses. They don't need them. I'm outta here. I have a nail to remove."

The leech blurred and blocked her way. "You can't leave. You need to know the truth."

She gasped. "Stop doing that. What the hell are you?"

"I already told you." He removed his

glasses. His eyes dilated into black holes, and his disgusting fangs protruded under his lips.

She yelped, staggering back, almost falling down.

He pulled back his human mask and shoved the glasses in his pocket. "I didn't mean to scare you. I never wanted you to see me like that until you'd made your choice, but I had to so you would believe me."

"What fucking choice?" she demanded incredulously.

"Please sit down so we can tell you the whole story." Asher brought a folded piece of paper out of his pocket and gave it to her. She flinched at first, but then she snatched it out his grip and unfolded it.

"That's me," she gasped again.

"This is Rena," he said.

The woman who started it all.

Two hundred and fifty years ago, a beautiful woman named Rena met a man named Alec. They fell in love. They were happy. Until a demon tore them apart. A vampire who claimed he loved her, too, and stole her away.

They didn't know Alec had a demon inside him as well. A beast that wouldn't be silenced. One horrific night, when everyone was drowning in their Halloween festivities, the beast roamed and found his mate in the arms of the vampire.

The two beasts fought over her, both sinking their fangs in her for a vicious claim.

Rena's unaccepting body couldn't take it and gave. Not turning into either monsters, she bled out in both their arms.

Desperate, the two beasts sought a witch for help. "Bring her back to life, and we will do anything," they had said.

The witch told them Rena came from a cursed bloodline, and she belonged to the devil now that she was dead. If they wanted to bring her back, they had to make a deal with him.

My brother and Asher shook hands with the devil that night, only to relive this tragedy every fifty years.

When Rena had to come back to life and choose a clan, then a mate by Halloween night.

Or else…

Of course, as they both perched down on the grass and wildflowers, the vampire was telling Belle the story from his side, where Alec was the one who stole Rena from him, not the other way around.

Alec's wolf breaths huffed closer. Then the unmistakable bone shattering pelted my ears.

His bare feet chomped the way from the forest to the clearing. "Don't believe a word he says. You've always been mine right from the start."

Asher jumped up. "Back off, Mutt. She loved me first. She just didn't tell you."

They pounced on each other and fought as humans. I didn't give a shit. I'd seen it a hundred times before. My concern was Belle. Her head jerked from one direction to another. She was silent the whole time, her heart skipping a beat after a beat, her eyes wide yet vacant.

She was in shock.

I examined her neck from where I stood. The two holes a vampire would crack were there, faded, almost healed, and so was Alec's mark.

They both had bitten her, and if Alec's story about this morning was true, then Belle was turning for real.

I folded my arms across my chest. "Would you stop fighting already? I'd like to know why you called for this meeting, Asher? And why you're expediting things like that, dumping everything on her all at once?"

"Yeah, why now, Parasite?" Alec punched the vampire's chest. "Because you fucking turned her!"

Asher replied with a shove on both my brother's shoulders. "It's your dumb ass who bit her first. I had to give her my venom to neutralize yours."

"What?" I questioned.

"You told me she wasn't turning that day, but she was. The hunger, the sex drive, the mark that hadn't faded, all details you've failed to notice while I have. Unlike you, I was saving her. Like always." Asher squared his shoulders, adjusting the sleeves of his suit jacket. "Belle is not turning, you idiots. She has both our venoms in her blood, giving her a hint of our powers for a short while until her blood is clean. Just like drugs."

The bloodsucker could be right. And until her blood is clean, if Belle didn't feed on blood, she wouldn't turn into a vampire. And if she didn't kill anyone—yeah, that was what it took to trigger the beast—she wouldn't turn into a shifter either.

"Is that why you're here? To show us what a fucking hero you are?" Alec scoffed. "What a way to do it, Leech, traumatizing an innocent woman like that."

"I called for this meeting because Damien Pattison finger fucked Belle!" Asher exploded.

"What the fuck? He's not allowed to touch her. Doesn't that break the deal as well, make him lose his claim on her forever?" I exclaimed.

The vampire clenched his fangs. "Practically, he didn't touch her. The devil went into her subconscious. He fucking made her like it."

My brother growled and howled and rumbled. Then he writhed and shifted into an angry wolf.

Instantly, my stare went to Belle. Her body became rigid, her lemur eyes on. A choked scream ripped through her chest, barely muffled behind her hand.

I saw the scene from her eyes for a moment. All she was seeing was a giant terror of fangs and claws and fur standing a few inches from where she sat. Then she screamed and screamed, collapsing onto the dirt.

"Isabella!"

Alec shifted back in a split-second. "Belle!"

I held a hand up, stopping them from running to her. "Damn it." I strode to her limp body and bent my ear to her chest. "She passed out. I'll take her home. Neither of you is allowed to touch her, to even see her until all this is sorted out."

CHAPTER 25
BELLE

Was it another daydream? A daynightmare was more like it. Vampires, werewolves and a devil after my cursed blood? I'd got to stop reading those books.

I opened my eyes to find myself tucked in my bed, and golden eyes glowing at me in the dark.

No no nonono. It wasn't a daynightmare. I was in one. Living it to the very core.

Panic surged through my legs. I stumbled

over the bed as I darted out of it, feet tangling in the loose sheets, screaming as I fell. "The fuck?!"

"Belle!"

In a flash, I picked myself up, darted to the bathroom and locked myself in there.

"Belle, wait. It's just me, Kayden." His voice came muffled behind the bathroom door.

"Go away. You're not real."

"Uh… Hate to disappoint you, Professor, but I am."

"You can't be." I seriously needed psychiatric help. But even if I went to therapy, what would I say? Monsters were real? They'd lock me up.

"Except that I am real. Alec, Asher and Pattison are, too," he said.

I crumbled to the cold tiles, my back against the door, terrified I'd been fucked up so badly I couldn't tell what was real anymore. I didn't know what was worse, my imagining supernatural beasts or for them to be real.

"Listen, Belle, I know you're afraid. You have every right," he said, his voice low and soothing—and right behind me, as if he was crouching next to the door at my level. "But you can choose to stick to what you've been taught in science books, ignore the truth and live with the irrevocable consequences…or you can open up your mind to accept there's another world out there so you can save yourself from a destiny worse than death."

Hot tears streamed down my face. I bent my knees up to my chest and buried my head between them. My mind raced, trying to make it all fit.

Maybe it did. All my unfathomed attraction to them, the need, the hunger, theirs and mine. That old connection I couldn't explain.

And their sizes and strength, their eyes, the way they spoke, their obsession with my smell and details, the bites, and the fucking eyes…

All the clues I'd chosen to ignore. *I just happened to be at the club where you celebrated your birthday. I guessed you liked cinnamon tea. I noticed you pressed your thumbnail.*

The blackout.

What happened at Damien's office.

No. It couldn't be true. How could I wrap my head around this madness?

"How did you get in my apartment, Kayden? How did I get in my apartment?"

"You passed out when you saw my brother's beast and the bloodsucker's fangs. I took you home and let us in using your keys."

"Of course."

"I'm never going to hurt you, Belle. I'm

here to look after you. The pack will look after you."

I knew that before he'd said it—more proof it was all real. My question was nothing but a useless evasion. I couldn't run anymore. I had to face my destiny. Whatever that was.

Hesitantly, I rose and cracked open the door. Kayden was standing with his hands braced on either side of the doorframe, his huge body blocking the path out of the bathroom as if making sure I wouldn't dart past him.

"You're hurting bad right now. I can feel that pain, can smell the hopelessness and the fear coming off you. And what's hurting and scaring you isn't an enemy I can offset. It's us." His gaze searched my face through the door's narrow opening. "But you're safe, Belle. I would do anything to prove it to you, just name it."

"I know you won't hurt me."

His face lit with a smile. "That's a good start. Would you please come out? The curious teacher in you wouldn't just meekly accept what she'd seen. You have all kinds of questions, and I'd be delighted to answer them."

I swung the door wider and stepped out. He cradled my face in his hands and gave me a hug. He was still shirtless, and I still had hungry wolf venom in my blood. I needed to end this embrace.

It wasn't an easy task, though. He looked exactly like Alec, equally steamy, and the idea of having sex with twins was a huge turn on for me. I felt his arms and back before I slightly drew away, but he was faster ending the hug.

He cleared his throat as I switched on the lights in the living room. Then he waited for me to sit before he helped himself to my kitchen and returned with a glass of water.

"Here." He gave it to me and took a seat. "What's the first thing you need to know?"

"Is it true what Joshua said? That I wouldn't turn?"

"Most likely. A wolf bite expedites vitalities in the body, causing excessive hunger, body growth, uncontrolled sex drive, anger issues, but a vampire's does the opposite. It numbs you, slows everything down, preserves you the way you are until you're literally dead. The two venoms work against each other, neutralizing the effects."

I loved the scientific explanations, the effort he exerted to make them. He cared enough to ease my mind the only way it could be eased.

"Unless…you complete the process," he added.

My breath strangled in my throat. "By drinking blood?"

He nodded. "Or killing a human."

My grip shook around the glass. I let the cold water soothe my dread a little.

Leaning forward, he held my shoulder. "I know what you're thinking, but I can assure you it's not so bad to turn into a shifter. The beast can be tamed."

"The beast, as in the humongous wolf I saw Alec become at the clearing? No, thanks."

He chuckled. "You won't be so reluctant when you try knotting."

My jaw fell, and heat assaulted my face. "Are you referring to…"

"Yes. It's much fucking hotter in reality than in the books you read."

My pussy clenched hard. *Imagine a cock swelling in your pussy, getting so big it's locked inside. You have all the pleasure you want as long as it takes, squeeze that big, fat cock to the last drop, and your pussy is filled with cum. And when you're all satisfied, you let the cock out.*

Pure, savage, raw hotness.

I bit my lip. Then I shook my head, yanking myself out of my sinful muses. I couldn't believe how easily sidetracked I was.

The world as I knew it was tumbling down, and all I was thinking about was kinky sex?

Damn you, wolf venom.

"And shifting isn't always bad. It can be fun," he continued.

"Fun? Looks like what you call a werewolf and what I call a werewolf are two completely different things."

He shrugged. "When the beast is tamed, you're in control. You can shift at will. You won't even turn on the full moon. A gift from the devil himself."

A shudder ran through me. "Damien Pattison?"

He nodded once.

My vision misted. A bigger shudder engulfed me. Then I couldn't control the tears. "The worst part is... he didn't force me."

"He was messing with your head."

"No," I blubbered through hiccupping breaths. "I kissed him first. I welcomed his touch." Embarrassment tore me apart, but I had to speak. "I liked it so fucking much."

"That's exactly what the devil does. Belle, it's okay. It's going to be okay."

"How is any of this okay? When I came here, I finally thought I was safe, starting a new life away from monsters and devils. Now look at me." I threw my hands in the air in exasperation and lifted my eyes to him. "I don't want to live like this, so lost, so afraid, knowing I will die when I'm fifty."

Silence fell heavy between us as he winced with my pain. "There must be a way out. Something to give the devil instead so he'd spare me."

"We tried everything. The more desperate we were, the more he was amused and insisted he would never back down on our deal."

"What if I don't choose at all , just walk away from all this?"

"You can't do that," he said it as a warning, disturbed. "You will die immediately and never come back. And he will claim your soul."

Tears hemorrhaged down my face. "I don't want to live the few years I have left as a monster, Kayden."

"Hey." He sat beside me and took me in his arms. "We'll make those years the best you will ever live. You'll be loved, happy and safe. Anything you need, anything you want will be yours."

That was beautiful, coming from him. The sincerity in his voice touched me, yet none of what he said soothed me. I raised my head off his chest; I was covering him with drool and snot. Then I dragged my palms away from his big muscles.

But our eyes locked, and I couldn't move an inch away. Instead of moving back, I was moving forward, and so was he. His lips closed the distance between us with a kiss.

They brushed against mine with softness that took me by surprise. He felt nothing like his brother. Although I thought Kayden as an alpha would be rougher than Alec in his passion, the way he was kissing me, taking his time, brushing and pressing with impeccable force proved me wrong.

He wasn't kissing me as someone he lusted after. This was a kiss of a man in love.

My heart fluttered, feeling every hidden pain that ever tormented his. Rena was his brother's mate, and he was in love with her. All these years, he'd been keeping it a secret, watching over and over again when someone else would claim her, while he had to pretend he had no feelings for her, even work to get her to another man.

His own twin.

Kayden stopped abruptly, his breaths harsh and hot against my wet lips. "I'm sorry. I'm so sorry." He fled out of our embrace and buried his face behind the bay window.

"It's okay," I whispered.

"No, it's not. You're Alec's mate. My brother's mate. You love each other. I should have never…" he growled, his fist clenched against the glass. "Please forgive me, Belle. It will never happen again."

I went to him and touched his shoulder. He flinched with a hiss as if my hand were made of fire. "Please…"

"You can hide it from anyone but not me."

"There's nothing to hide. That was just…a mistake. It means nothing at all. Any man, seeing a woman that vulnerable, could make such a mistake. Don't make a big deal out of it."

I ignored his unsuccessful attempt to hurt and push me away. "Have you ever told Rena that you love her?"

His head jerked at me, and his eyes burned with the golden gleam. "No. Because I do not love her."

Courage possessed me as I dared move closer to this incredible body, not run from the beast eyes. "Well…poor, Rena."

"Why…" he swallowed. "Why are you saying that?"

Watching this huge man stammering and sweating as I approached him built up my desire for him. Heat came up—and down—in waves. I couldn't not touch him. My arms snaked around his back, and I let my body press against his.

"Please stop moving, Professor."

"Why? Because you won't be able to stop yourself from touching me?"

"Yes, and it won't be just touching."

The friction between our hips was a delight yet a cruel tease. The bulge in his jeans was big, but I knew how much bigger it could get. I wanted to—had to— know how hard he would get for me.

"Don't you want to know why I felt sorry for Rena?"

He barely nodded.

My breasts were now on his ribs, and my hands were sliding to the hard V down his hips that led straight to everything I wanted at this moment. "Because she loved you, too, Kayden."

The golden strikes flamed. His erection doubled, poking me in the stomach. "No. She loved Alec. Only Alec."

"I can feel everything she's ever felt. I am her after all, and I can tell you beyond any doubt, Rena loved all three of you."

"Three?"

"Joshua, Alec and you."

He looked as if I'd stabbed him in the back.

"This can't be. No woman loves three men at once, and certainly not that combination. A twin wolf and a vamp? That's sick."

"I'm going to borrow your words, *Wolf*. You can choose to stick to what you've been taught, ignore the truth and live with the miserable consequences…or you can open up your mind to accept there's another world out there, a woman's world where there is room for more than one man, and save yourself the misery of a torn heart." My palms left his front and dipped in the back pockets of his jeans. "Oh fuck me."

"What?"

"Nothing! I didn't say anything!"

His cock throbbed on my belly. "You said fuck me."

"Yeah? Well, I…I wanted to say something and forgot what it was so I said, *oh fuck me*, as in…*oh fuck me, I forgot*, not *oh fuck me, Kayden, please. Your ass is so hot, and I'm so fucking wet for you I need you to fuck me. Here. Now.*"

A growl ripped out of him painfully. "Because that would have been completely inappropriate, Professor."

I pushed myself more into his erection and squeezed his ass harder. "I know. So inappropriate."

The devil's words thundered in my head,

yelling over everything else. He told me I deserved to be happy. He told me to take what was mine.

Joshua was mine. Alec was mine.

And Kayden was mine.

Everything about him said it for him, and the way I felt—the way Rena felt—confirmed it. The three of them loved her, and she loved them back.

So did I.

"Can I use your bathroom?" he requested.

I blinked and raised my brows. It must have taken me a while to respond because he repeated his request with an impatient expression. "Oh, yeah. Sure. I just…I wasn't expecting that…now."

He practically sprinted to the bathroom. The door squeaked but didn't shut. I went over there and saw him leaning into the tiled wall. "Are you okay?"

"I have a huge hard-on aching in my pants. I really need to jack my dick raw before I do something stupid, something that rips a family apart."

"I don't know how to respond to that." I blinked again. "Is that why you need the bathroom? To…jerk off?"

"Yes, but then I thought it wasn't nice to do it in someone else's bathroom, not without them knowing."

Jizz etiquette from Kayden Beastly. Do not do it in a stranger's bathroom without their consent first. That totally makes it okay.

Laughter took over me, and he looked at me, puzzled. "What?" he asked gruffly, and I laughed harder. His hands fell to his hips as he spun to face me. "Can I do it here or what?"

I chopped off the giggles the second his massive erection stared me in the face. "No."

"Shit." He sighed and looked away.

"You can't do it in the bathroom because it's too small to fit us both...and I want to watch."

CHAPTER 26
BELLE

Kayden resisted fiercely. Watching him, his cock, coming for me would still hurt his brother.

It got nothing out of me but a giggle. As if Kayden hadn't been jerking off to me for years already. Wouldn't that hurt Alec, too? Or keeping it a secret where no one watched made it better?

I didn't see the logic in that. Besides, I was the one who wanted to watch. Kayden wasn't offering anything, so he could just pretend I wasn't there and do his thing.

His resistance faded. He wanted this as much as I did.

We went back to the living room. He took the armchair and I the sofa bed. He unbuttoned his jeans and worked the zipper. I licked my lips, compulsively, my eyes wide with anticipation.

"This is wrong, Belle."

"Please, call me Professor."

"Fuck," he growled. I loved that sound from him. Much different from Alec's feral growl. With Kayden, it came out more natural, tormented even. He couldn't help it. And that alone was sexier than watching the twin of my future mate masturbate.

His hands were not pulling his cock out. Was he going to change his mind? Damn it. I was painfully wet, and if he wouldn't stick his huge cock in me, the least he could do was let me touch myself while I watched his cum melting down his long shaft. Maybe let me lick it too?

My nipples hardened to the point of pain. I took off my top, skirt and bra, forgetting all about my scarred body and self-conscious. My breasts tumbled free, and I sighed in relief. That felt so good. I'd been wearing that thing all day my back, neck and chest were killing me. I couldn't wait to get out of it.

"What the fuck are you doing?" he protested.

"It's my apartment. I'll do whatever I want. I can't stay in that fucking bra any second longer. It's not like you haven't seen them before." I lay down and stretched my legs. Keeping my wet panties on, I enjoyed the way his eyes flicked with hunger at the sight of my nakedness. "By the way, what did Alec say to that?"

"Nothing," he mumbled, his lips twitching.

"If you say so." I took a deep breath. The smell of my own wetness induced a moan out of my throat. I wondered what it must have been doing to him. That was a lot of self-control he had not to flip and hump me all night by now. As painful as it was for me—my pussy—I respected the great lengths he would go for his brother.

"Could you not make that sound?"

I moaned again. "This sound?"

His head tilted back to the ceiling as he swore again.

"I need to get off, Kayden. You can see how hard my nipples are and can smell how wet my pussy is, and it's all for you. So it's either you do this harmless thing you probably do every day, and we'll both be a little more happy, or—since you put my potential mates on a timeout—Pornhub for me tonight."

"You watch porn?"

"Mostly read it, but yeah. What? Men can live on it, and nobody bats an eye, but when a woman does it, you look like that?"

He scowled and scratched his chin. Then he just sighed.

"What's it going to be? Coming to strangers with big fat cocks or one sexy as fuck wolf?" I asked with that voice of the sexual deviant possessing me.

Without another word, he dug his hand in his jeans and freed his huge erection.

I persuaded him like the devil persuaded me. Or was that Damien's work all along?

Are you still in my head, Damien? Are you here, watching, touching your filthy dick?

I know you are.

Why don't you show yourself, coward?

Silence answered me. Of course.

Kayden took his hand away, giving me a full view. His cock jutted hard from his pelvis, pre-cum glistening on the big tip, sinews throbbing along the sides.

My lips parted as my chest heaved with labored breaths. "You do have identical dicks." If Alec could do this awesome shit to me on that night, how about having double that fun? Throw some vampire roughness in there with a lot of biting…

I moaned loudly as if I was eating a delicious dessert.

"You're driving me insane with those moans," he said.

I smiled. "Have you ever done this with Rena or any of her versions?"

He shook his head slowly.

"Would you guide me, tell me what you'd like me to do to my body while you *jack your dick raw*?"

A groan echoed out of his chest. "That's not what they do on Pornhub."

My smile grew into a grin. "I'm having a live show. I might as well use the perks."

His glowing eyes pierced me, eating me up. "You don't know how much it's taking me not to rip those panties off and sit you on this cock you love so much."

"I know. It's turning me on even more."

He sighed. "It's also so hard for me to know you need something and I can't give it to you."

"All I need you to do is tell me how to touch myself…for you."

His gaze roamed my body from head to toe, then it lingered on my breasts. "Play with your tits for me, Professor."

The gruff voice and the blazing need made it so much hotter than how I'd have imagined something like that. I cupped my breasts, one in each palm, squeezed and massaged them before rubbing gently across the engorged nipples. I moaned again.

His fist wrapped around his shaft and, using his thumb, he swirled the spilling pre-cum on the head of his beast cock and pinched it between his fingers. "Yeah, Professor, that's it. Make it feel good."

Shit, that was super sexy. I kept up the fondling, stopping to pinch and rub the nipples. My eyes closed as I bit down on my lip. Each time I pinched my hard nipples, a jolt of pleasure raced down my belly and between my legs. "Do you like that?"

There was a light jiggle. "So fucking much."

I opened my eyes, and he was rubbing his cock slowly, his hand hitting the jeans button, causing the jiggle.

With every pinch and squeeze of mine, his strokes moved faster. My hips bucked up and down, my legs spreading wider.

"You're squirming. Want to touch that wet pussy, Professor?"

I nodded with a groan.

He lowered his jeans and boxers. His balls

came into sight, and he gave them a light squeeze and push with his other hand. "Move your panties to the side and spread your legs. I want to watch your pussy all wet first."

My body burned with his orders and the added scorching view of his engorged balls. "Do you want me to take them off instead?"

"No," he pleaded. "Your panties are the last thing that's keeping me in my chair."

I did as he wanted. Pushed my drenched underwear to the side, put one leg down, the other on the back of the sofa bed, giving him a nice view of my opening dripping with the juices he induced.

"Oh fuck. FUCK!" His teeth speared his lips as his fist moved fast up and down his thick, long cock. "Rub that pussy for me."

I started with light strokes on my outer lips. They were soaking wet and the juices slid down the insides of my thighs. With the hand that kept the panties to the side, I traced through the warm slickness running down my skin. Kayden growled, flexing his hips.

My fingers on my pussy reached my clit and rubbed it in circles. His watching and growling made it even hotter. And…knowing that Damien, too, was watching without showing himself set another gush between my legs.

It was sick and wrong and dark to fantasize about the devil himself, but I liked it. So fucking much. I moaned and whimpered and writhed all over the sofa bed.

"You're so hot, Professor," Kayden groaned. "All these juices should be in my mouth. I would drink you to the last drop until you came, then I'd eat you even harder so you'd come again on my tongue."

"Oh, Kayden," I cried out, so close. "I want us to come together. Can you do that for me?"

"Yes, baby. I'm only holding off so you'd come first. Put those fingers inside your pussy."

Baby. Kayden called me baby. A smile stretched my lips as I slipped a finger inside of me, and then another. My ass lifted up as I fucked myself while the devil watched in the dark. And the enormous werewolf, my student, the twin of my possible mate, jerked off to the scene. It was erotic and filthy and wrong and so fucking hot. It didn't take long before I was screaming out in a mind-blowing orgasm, the best I'd ever given myself. "Now, Kayden. Now!"

"Look at me! I'm coming…thinking only of you, watching you, coming only for you, Professor."

I watched as his fist moved frantically around his cock, and it jerked. Hard. My breathing and pulse kicked up, my own orgasm rippling inside me. The first jet that shot from his cock arched high and landed on the floor by my foot. Then he groaned my name with each following spurt, all six of them.

I screamed with him as my climax ended. My eyes held his glowing ones, my breaths only gasps. "That was beautiful."

"Beautiful?"

Watching a man this big come that hard for me was beautiful and sinfully delicious. "Yes."

A faint smile crossed his face. "You're beautiful."

"Would you sleep here with me tonight?"

"Belle…"

"Just sleep. You can keep your boxers on."

"Just sleep?"

I nodded. "I just don't want to be alone with my head tonight. I'll feel safer with you around."

CHAPTER 27
BELLE

The familiar buzz of my alarm woke me. Crap. I forgot to turn that thing off for good. It wasn't like I was going back to that university of hell any time soon. Not with the devil himself as my boss. I couldn't just waltz in, pretending it was all a hallucination. Besides, Damien only hired me because he was after my soul—and pussy.

A shudder ran through me, but I luxuriated in the delicious sensation of waking up with Kayden's massive body serving as both my pillow and my bed. He smelled so warm, so good. The heavy weight of one of his arms slung across my back, the fingers of his opposite hand curled around my thigh—as if he'd fallen asleep while holding me and never let me go.

I knew I'd slept like a baby in his arms, after that orgasm.

Speaking of orgasms, hello, morning semi-erections. His huge thingy peeked from his boxers and rubbed at my thigh. It was tempting to do stuff I wasn't supposed to, but I had to respect him as much as he respected me and his brother.

I dragged myself out of bed, my inner devil, not Damien, whispering foul thoughts in my ears. The things I would do with that cock. I was dying to taste it, see how much of it I can put in my mouth before it fucked my throat.

Fuck manners.

I shook my head as I took one final glance at Kayden before I yanked my gaze to the windows. The sunlight flooded the room. Why the hell hadn't I bought those curtains yet? I hoped the sun wouldn't wake Kayden. He looked so peaceful.

The bed creaked under him. "I love you, Belle."

My heart skipped a beat. I spun at him. His

eyes were still closed. His breathing gained its sleep rhythm back.

He must have been dreaming when he said it. My heart fluttered at the sweetness. "I love you, too," I whispered. "All three of you."

I was in love with three men. No, three beasts.

I didn't know which part was worse, the fact that my heart was split three ways or that my lovers were werewolves and vampires.

The answer came loud and clear in my head.

Neither.

Beasts or not, I was in love with them, and they loved me back. That put a smile on my face. Nothing that terrible could make someone this happy, right?

What was terrible was me having only twenty-two more years to live.

That was what I should have been worrying about, and the fact that I had to choose one of my three beasts to spend those remaining years with by Halloween.

To think I'd come to Forest Grove to leave all my worries and problems behind and finally have peace away from monsters…

My shoulders slumped as I walked out of the bedroom and into the bathroom. I washed the sleep off me, and when I came out,

Kayden was in the living room.

I jumped. "You spooked me."

"Sorry. Good morning." His gruff voice was raw with sleep and full of masculinity. It went straight to my pussy.

"Good morning. You need the bathroom?"

"To wash my face, nothing else."

I laughed under my breath. "And maybe pee. You look like you need it."

"No, baby. That's all you. Get used to it if you ever ask me to sleep next to you all night again."

He moved past me, his front brushing against mine, and a delicious shiver ripped through me. "Sorry, your place is so tiny."

I heard him chuckle in the bathroom as I plopped on the nearest seat. Looking down, I saw my nipples through my nightgown. If we stayed like this—I in the thin thing, him in boxers—what he was avoiding last night could be inevitable now.

I donned a robe and a fresh pair of underwear that would soak up pretty soon. "You put my potential mates on a timeout, yes?!"

"Yup!"

I tied the robe and headed back to the armchair. "When does that end?"

"When your blood is clean." He got out of

the bathroom, his face and hair dripping water on his naked chest. "Do you have a towel? I'd have loved to use yours, but I didn't want to without asking you first."

That was so intimate. "You can use it."

He vanished into the bathroom, and I smiled.

"Coffee?" He came back all dry.

I nodded. "About the timeout, I get that Alec must listen to you because you're Alpha, but why would Joshua? He comes from a different clan."

He didn't answer and entered the kitchen. "You seem to know so much about clans for a skeptic, for someone that passed out when they saw a shift."

"You wouldn't believe the amount of information I have."

"Where did you get it? Your porn books?"

I giggled. "Yes."

The smell of hot coffee nourished my senses as he emerged into the living room. He handed me a cup. "You're asking about Alec and the leech because you miss them or your pussy does?"

"Both. If I turn into a shifter, I'd be a bunny instead of a wolf. My sex drive certainly supports that conclusion."

He sipped at his own cup. "I thought you'd

make a cute lemur."

"What? Is that because of my big eyes?"

"Yup. They go so big when you're staring, it's so cute."

Hearing that word coming from this face, out of this body sent more giggles out of my throat.

"What's so funny?"

"You said cute."

He looked at me, perplexed. Then he shook his head and grabbed the jeans he left on the floor last night. "I'm going to get us some breakfast. I bet you're hungry."

My stomach growled on cue. "Starving. But how are you going out like this? Don't you need a shirt or something?"

"Not in Forest Grove." He winked at me as he buttoned his jeans. "It's not like I can wear any of your blouses anyway."

As he headed out, he stopped in his tracks and leaned on the front door frame. "Is it weird that I'm not jealous?"

"Of?"

"Alec and Asher. The way you want them. The way you want the three of us."

"Not to me."

He smirked and shut the door behind him.

Oh, Kayden, why do you have to be so dreamy?

I wished the other two would have been as

levelheaded as this wolf. Especially, when they knew how I felt about having to choose.

I went over to my phone and checked my messages. I'd found two from Detective Magnolia. She was assigned to my case from the beginning. Had they set a verdict date already?

Coffee filled my mouth as I tapped to listen. "Professor Ferro, this is Detective Magnolia. I'm afraid I have some bad news." There was a pause, and an ominous chill ran through my body. "Montgomery has escaped…"

I choked on my coffee, my eyes bulging painfully in their cavities. She was talking some more, but I couldn't listen. Swiftly, I threw my phone on the table, grabbed the TV remote and switched it on the News.

A reporter stood opposite to my old house with a red strip under her.

Beast Escape before Verdict.

"Professor Declan Montgomery, known as the Beast from the Beauty and the Beast domestic violence case has escaped last night…"

The reporter's voice droned. Every rational thought torn apart. Only desperation left.

I hurled my cup across the TV. Brown liquid spilled on the smashed screen, the cup in pieces all over the room. Terror shredded me open, ripping a scream from my throat.

I was a sobbing wreck on the floor when Kayden came running through the door. "Belle!" He'd thrown the bags in his hands and collected me into his arms.

"He's out. He escaped. He's out." I trembled. Quaked.

He looked around for a second, and then he hugged me closer. "Oh, baby. Baby, no. You're safe. As long as we're here, you're safe."

I shook my head in a manic frenzy.

"Look at me! Look at me, Belle." He cradled my face in his hands. "He can't get anywhere near you. We're here now. He can't hurt you."

Kayden couldn't stop what was hurting me. All that pain. All that agony that wouldn't leave me be. Nothing could.

Mindless panic took over me again. I had to get away. To never let that monster find me. Screaming, I lurched out of Kayden's grip for the open door. Dashing over one flight of stairs after another, I leapt down and down until I landed on the sidewalk outside my apartment building. Then I sprinted away from the horror that awaited me, as if running fast enough and far enough would stop it from ever catching me.

I crossed to the woods, Kayden's shouts after me. The trees lashed at my face, the dirt digging under my toenails as I ran. It wasn't long before I'd collapsed, and Kayden was on top of me.

"Please, baby. You can't be that afraid of that fucker, not when we're all here for you. The whole pack not just Alec and I. Even Asher. We can protect you. From anything."

"Where were you when I needed it?"

"You know we couldn't or—"

"The devil would have me. Well, I have news for you. The devil did have me, Kayden. For ten fucking years. And now he's back for me."

CHAPTER 28

BELLE

Forest Grove police officers swarmed in my apartment and around the building. Joshua sat with me while they kept telling me not to worry and they had it under control.

Kayden and Alec stood against the living room wall, arms crossed over their chests. I'd told them to go before the police asked them for a justifiable reason they were at my place. But the wolf twin had invited over their bear brothers and told the police they could all help patrolling the neighborhood.

"Your students really care for you, Professor Ferro," one of the officers had said. I couldn't decide whether he was being nice or just mocking me.

Even if he was one of those people I was afraid would turn on me if any rumors had spread about me screwing around, I didn't care. The monster was already out. The worst had happened. I had nothing more to fear.

Detective Magnolia had flown to Oregon and arrived at my place around nightfall. I didn't know what hour exactly; it was hard to look at clocks when time was another monster moving slowly and rapidly at once. Every second fell heavily as it delayed the inevitable or brought me closer to my awful destiny.

"A police car will be outside your building at all times. An officer will escort you to campus, too," she said.

"No need. I'm not going back to work," I replied, my mind spiraling.

"Sure. Take a few days off—"

"I'm not going back. Ever."

"You just started your job. Why would you say that? Did something happen?"

I exchanged a glance with the boys.

"Did Montgomery threaten you while he was in jail? Did you know anything about his escape?" she pressed.

"What? No! Why are you interrogating me?"

"I'm not." Her voice softened. "But, Isabella, if you know anything, you have to tell me. Anything at all can help us capture him and put him back where he belongs."

"I'm not going back to work because my boss is the devil, and I'm sick and tired of working with monsters from hell, not because I know anything about Declan or his escape." I darted to my room before I'd explode.

I felt as if I was shattered into a million volatile pieces inside one vessel, awaiting to erupt. When I'd no longer be.

No more Declan. No more cursed blood. No more devils.

Just peace.

"Why did she say her boss was the devil? I'm sure you know something. If you're really looking after her, you must speak." The detective's voice reached me clearly, not even muffled behind my closed bedroom door.

Damn it. I shouldn't have said anything.

I stood by the door in anticipation, only negative hums echoing.

"Professor Asher, you work with Isabella closely?" she asked.

"I do," Joshua answered.

"Have you noticed any change in her behavior in the past week or so?"

There was a pause and then a sigh. "A couple of days ago, she was agitated. Then she stopped coming to class."

What the fuck?

"Have you contacted her to know the reason behind that?"

"Listen, Detective. Sexual harassments aren't easy to prove. Especially, when the woman is involved in a case such as Isabella's. She didn't want to say anything or press any charges. It's her word against his. She couldn't risk the fuss another charge would create. With the verdict coming out in a few days, she chose to remain silent so she wouldn't jeopardize anything."

I threw my head between my hands and cried. Why would he say this shit now? Did I really need to start another war…with the fucking devil?

A grunt.

Another sigh.

Silence.

Why isn't anybody saying anything no more?

"Thank you, Professor, for your time," she said.

That's it?

Looks like I was worried for no reason. Thank

you, Joshua, for your lie. It shut her up.

A knock on my door made me flinch. "Isabella?" she called out.

I rotated the knob slowly and met her gaze with weeping eyes. "Yes?"

"Stay strong, Professor. You're in good company here. We won't stop until we find him, and you're safe again."

CHAPTER 29

JOSHUA

Three weeks had passed, and the son of a bitch hadn't shown himself yet. The police were getting tired. The patrol car was pulled out. Even though the fugitive was never found or captured trying to escape borders, the police strongly believed he didn't break out of prison to come after Isabella; he escaped because he was guilty and only wanted to flee the country, if he hadn't already.

I didn't care about the police leaving. We

were more capable of protecting her than any human.

I, alone, was.

But to tell her she didn't need any shifters around was only going to add to her distress. They made her feel safer when they were around. That was all that mattered.

We worked as a hive around her, in harmony as though we were best friends, not eternal enemies— even the brown bears got along with us— and she was our queen.

A tired and sad queen.

My gaze drifted to her as she stood by the bay windows of her bedroom. She still looked so damn beautiful, but I hated to see her like this. Hollows in her cheeks. Her clothes hung off her body loosely as if she had been on one of those trendy diets. A diet might carve away the softness in her cheeks, but it sure as hell didn't put those shadows in her eyes or give her the haunted, hunted look she couldn't manage to conceal.

That bloody Montgomery had been consuming her from the inside out for the past three weeks. I wished she could have understood that whatever he would do, it didn't matter. He wouldn't get anywhere near her. If he even thought about it, I would take him out in no time. I would be there to help her through whatever she was going through. We all were.

Yet nothing had convinced her to stop being afraid. He had tampered with her mind severely. The psychological tricks he had worked on her were worse than magic. She needed a lot more time to heal than what was given to her.

"Admiring the curtains, Professor?" Alec joked—bragged.

Kayden slapped the back of his twin's head. "Not because you bought the fucking curtains, you get to mention them every five minutes."

"Quit picking on each other." She dropped the edge of the curtain. "As much I love your taste, no. I'm cursing at the ass of the last officer walking away. How could they leave like that? Declan must be watching, waiting for them to leave so he can pounce."

"They weren't doing much. We're better off without them." Alec left his brother's side on the floor and stood.

"Yeah. They're full of shit. I can't buy that the fucker didn't escape to have Belle back." Kayden rose, too, and they both flanked her as she walked to her bed. "If you had given anything with his smell, we would have tracked him down for you and brought him to his knees at your feet."

"I didn't take anything when I left, not even my old clothes. I didn't want anything to remind me of him or my old life," she said.

"I just don't understand why he hasn't made a move yet? It doesn't make any sense," Alec said.

"Psychological warfare." Isabella swallowed and glanced at me as I leaned against her dresser. "He's failed to kill me the last time he tried. Now he's doing it slowly, until I break and go find him myself to beg him to stop."

I straightened up. "That will never happen. Not on my watch."

Alec glared at me. "Not on *our* watch."

"I told you to stop picking on each other. That includes Joshua," she said.

"But—"

"No buts." She wet her lips as she lay down on the bed. The wolves set pillows behind her back and sat on either side of her. "Look, there's something that I need to discuss with you. I've been putting it off for so long with everything that's happening, but now is the time." She held Alec's gaze. "But you have to promise me to stay calm and understand that this's really how I feel and what I want."

He held her hand. "Anything you want is

yours, sweetheart."

"*Our* sweetheart," I retorted.

"That's precise. This is exactly what I want to say." She glanced at Kayden for a few moments, longer than usual. Then she held his hand.

His lips shivered. "Belle."

"No," Alec growled and darted off the bed. "You can't… This is…" His fists clenched and unclenched. Then his fingers turned into claws.

I blurred to stand between Isabella and him. "Hey, you need to calm down."

"Stay out of it, Parasite. This is between me and my fucking brother."

Kayden jumped in front of me and held Alec's shoulders. "You need to listen. Nothing happened. I never betrayed you. It's not what you think."

Alec jerked off Kayden's hands and howled, shifting in the middle of the room. His tail swung, pushing things off on the floor. He snarled and moved like a rabid dog, breaking furniture right and left.

The hair on my body pricked. Instinct took over and fangs came out.

"No, no, no!" Isabella was on her feet, staring the wolf in the eye, tears in hers. "You can't do this."

I spread an arm in front of her. "Isabella, stay back."

"I'm not afraid of you, any of you. Not anymore." She passed me and crouched down to the wolf's level. She reached a hand at his head, and I yelled my protest. Ignoring me, she touched the furry skull.

Despite the huffing and puffing and ugly, drooling, clenched jaws, she embraced the wolf and rested her forehead on his. "I'm in love with you as much as you are in love with me. All three of you."

He snarled again and slid his head under her arms, leaving her embrace. She sighed, shoulders slumping. "Kayden pushed me away as far as he could, Alec. He never touched me because of his love for you. But this isn't about either of you. Or about Joshua. It's about me. About Rena."

"What about Rena? I asked.

She wiped her eyes. "You think she loved you first, and when she knew about what you were, she went to Alec. But that's not true."

"What do you mean? This is exactly what happened." I glanced from her to Kayden, who was eerily silent, the dead muscles of my heart suddenly felt so cold.

"I'm sorry, Joshua. It was Kayden she fell for first," she said.

"What?" My shout died in Alec's howl.

"She loved Kayden, and Kayden loved her. But he knew his brother wanted her so he never spoke of his love. Not even to himself. Rena left and met you, fell for you, but then she got scared when she found out you were a vampire. Destiny led her back where Alec and Kayden were, and Alec won her over with his deep love."

Dazed, I leafed through the memories. Could this be true? She hadn't told me about Kayden the same way she hadn't told Alec about me?

Alec shifted back. He stayed on all fours, covering his naked junk. "All this time, she wanted him. She only came to me because I looked like him."

"No," Belle said. "She loved you. You, Alec. And I do, too. The only difference between Rena and me is that she loved all three of you at separate intervals of time. But I love you separately and together all at the same time."

"If that's true, what are you going to do when you have to make the choice?" Alec asked for all of us.

"I don't know, but can't we, at least till that day comes, try to have a glimpse of peace, a glimpse of happiness together? I'm so tired of being miserable and afraid all the time."

An angry scowl contorted his face. "Is that what you really want?"

"Yes. It's what I need. I desperately need this, Alec," she sobbed, and then she looked up at Kayden and me. "Please don't make me choose. Not now. I'm not ready to give any of you up. I just can't."

"I think you've already made your choice." Alec growled and shifted out of the apartment.

CHAPTER 30

KAYDEN

I shifted and followed my brother into the woods. I had to make him listen. Understand.

I had to bring him back to her.

Running in the dark, I trailed him to the willow tree. He just stood there, howling. My paws treaded carefully toward him. His snarls stopped me in my tracks.

His pain led to mine. His anger I couldn't bear. It was all my fault. I had to find a way to rectify all this.

Alec, please. I know how mad you are at me. You have every right. I made a terrible mistake. Tell me how to fix it. What can I do for you to forgive me?

You are my brother. My twin. You were supposed to help me win her over, protect her from the vampire so I could claim her. Not you.

I haven't claimed her.

That's even worse.

I tilted my head in confusion.

Had you claimed her, I would have been able to pour all my rage on you. I would have had the right to be mad at you. His jaws clenched hard. *But you…you fucking fell in love with her.* He let out a bellowing howl and shifted back. "If I stay in this form another second I won't be able to stop myself from hurting you."

I had to shift, too, so he could hear me when I talked. "Take a swing if it will make you feel better. I deserve it."

"Fuck you." He kicked at the dirt and dropped under the tree. "Always trying to be the better beast."

"I'm not trying to be anything. I just want you to be happy."

"Happy? Giving up your girl is supposed to make me happy? You're my brother. I fucking love you, too. You really think I'm that selfish to take a mate knowing she is yours even if I really want her?"

"Rena was never mine. I never told her anything." Taking a look back, I saw now it was a mistake. My biggest regret ever. Perhaps… If I'd just told her, I might have been able to save her life. The vampire wouldn't have been in her life. Alec wouldn't have fought him that night. She wouldn't have died. No devil. No curse. Alec would have found another mate. And all of us would have lived our happily ever after.

"All this time… I mean, I'm not blind. I see the way you've always looked at her. But I thought you only saw her as a breeder. Not a mate. But you've been fucking in love with her. Right from the beginning. That makes *me* the bad guy here."

Guilt hit me hard. "You're not. This is all my fault."

He shook his head. "Your fault, my fault, it doesn't matter. Blame won't fix anything. All that matters now is her. Just go back to Belle, Kayden. She needs you."

"She needs you, too."

A bitter laugh erupted out of him. "Not one of the previous versions dared share what Belle shared about Rena's heart. What does that tell you, Brother?"

"That she really needs the three of us." I squatted and met his glowing eyes. "Like you said, she is all that matters now. You have to be there for her. It's how we're wired, Alec. You cannot bail on your mate."

"She's not my mate. Not this time." He shrugged. "Maybe I'll have a better shot next time. Or not. I really don't know how to look at Rena now."

"No, Alec. Nothing has changed. She's always loved you. She still does. Your history together, your feelings for each other all these years can't be erased like that."

"I can't. Watching her be split three ways… I just can't." He held on to the tree trunk and rose.

I straightened my back. "You'd rather live without her than share her?"

His eyes blazed in the dark. "Just don't let the parasite have her."

He shifted and ran off.

CHAPTER 31
JOSHUA

"Do you think I've lost him?" Isabella whispered in my arms.

She had been crying silently since the wolves left, and I didn't know how to react but to put all my pain and confusion aside, and embrace her.

Holding her in my arms in her bed, listening to her mesmerizing heartbeat, knowing she was safe was everything to me. I understood she was dealing with feelings she didn't comprehend since we met, and the

Declan situation had made her more confused.

But she was mine. Isabella and I belonged together. Even if she didn't believe in fate or soul mates, it was the only way to explain this power, this connection I'd felt from the first moment I saw her. Not only in this life, but since the very first one. We were lost souls that had found each other in the dark. Our lives wouldn't make sense alone. Not mine, at least.

I was tired of playing games, of pretending I didn't mind the wait or the rivalry. I wanted her for myself. Forever.

I couldn't care less for her question. "Even if you have, you still have me." *I* was here. All she needed was right here next to her. I leaned in for a kiss to show her I'd been waiting for so long, and I was never going to let go of what was mine. To make her feel how much I needed her warmth, her heart.

Suddenly, she pulled back from my embrace. "Can vampires breed?"

I was stunned for a moment. I certainly didn't expect that. "Not if both parents are vampires. Why do you ask?"

"Do you not think I need to know something like that before I make my choice?"

I felt as though all blood had rushed out of my body, except that I didn't have any. "I thought you weren't going to make one now."

"Looks like I have to."

"No, you don't." I couldn't believe I'd just said that, but anything was better than the alternative. Basing her decision on procreation meant one thing. I lost before I even tried.

And if she didn't choose me in this life, I didn't know what to do with myself. Suddenly, no patience was left in me, and I had grown awfully tired of the waiting game.

"Either way, I need to gather enough information for that night," she said.

A lump clogged my throat. "Is that really how you're going to rule out options? Scientifically?"

"Do you have a better method? I'm open to any suggestions because I have no clue how to choose between three men I love to death. Three stubborn beasts that would rather tear each other than live together for a few weeks with the woman they say they love." Tears welled up in her eyes. "If you guys can't let me have you now, then I might as well make my choice already."

"And children matter to you that much? Even though they are going to be *beasts* like their fathers, and you wouldn't have a lot of time with them?"

Pain etched on her face. I was sorry I had to be an asshole and remind her of all these predicaments. It was my last resort to change her mind. Perhaps my last chance to win with her.

She sat up, her long hair brushing against my forearm before taking away the warmth and cascading behind her back instead. "Do you know why and how Declan tried to kill me?"

No. I wasn't sure I needed to know, either. My wrath was the hardest to control. If I listened in her own words the details of the terrors that piece of shit had imposed on her, I would roam this earth until I found him and sank my fangs into his throat, drinking his filthy blood to the last drop.

I would have loved to do such a thing, but if for any reason, I was tied to his pathetic demise, she would be, too. That I couldn't chance.

"Ten days before the incident, I found out I was…" She lifted her chin, fighting her tears. "I found out I was pregnant. It was the first good news I'd received since I was forced to leave school and kept a prisoner at my own house for over a year. I shouldn't have been that happy, knowing I was carrying a monster's baby, tying myself forever to that horrible person. But I was.

"I kept the news to myself for a week, thinking if I should tell him ever. I should have just run away, but I was afraid he would hurt me and the baby if I did. I convinced myself that if I told him, he would be happy too and finally change." She chuckled as tears rolled down her cheeks. "Could you believe how ridiculously silly and naive I had been?"

"Isabella…you must stop blaming yourself."

"Never. I will always blame myself," she fumed. "I put myself and my child in the custody of a very dangerous man. A monster who beat the crap out of me the second he knew, kicking my belly, calling me a bitch, throwing me off the stairs until I was bleeding everywhere." Her arms circled her abdomen as she sniveled and quivered. "Then he put me into a hospital unconscious. I woke up, and it was all gone."

"Gone?"

"My baby was gone. The hospital report was gone. Apparently, I had been such a klutz as always and fell down the stairs when Declan wasn't home. He saved me just in time and had been waiting all night at the hospital for me to wake up. The loving husband had even brought me fucking flowers."

"The sick bastard," I groaned, picturing his ripped head off his neck.

"I screamed at him, yelling at the top of my lungs what he'd done, threatening I'd go to the police. He just smiled and warned me the next time it wouldn't be a hospital where he'd put me, it would be the psych ward." Her hands balled into fists so tight her knuckles became white. "You were never pregnant, Belle. It was all in your head," she mocked a man's voice.

"I got out of the hospital determined on one thing. Run." The tears froze in the corners of her bloodshot eyes. "I beat myself for it every day. I can't believe I had to lose a baby to snap out of his prison."

I held her arms, rubbing them gently. "The important thing is that you did. You had the courage to leave."

"But not enough intelligence not to get caught. He found me after one day. One pathetic day," she mused. "Then he killed me. He tortured me for one night, said I wasn't worth any more of his time, and he just stabbed me with a knife at a crappy motel."

My eyes squeezed shut. My fingers curled tightly around her flesh. Just tearing his throat to drink his disgusting blood wasn't going to cut it. I could hear my fist smashing into that Declan's nose, shattering his bones, splattering red blood on the dirty walls of whatever hole he'd locked himself in. I could see the man's blood dropping through the tiniest bites around his body, in a slow, agonizing death, in my mind.

"*Might as well have one last fuck with you* was the last thing I heard him say before I felt myself going cold, my breathing erratic," she continued. "I retreated into the darkness, not wanting another moment of this. Even when I was dying, I couldn't catch a break. The last thing my bleeding out body would experience was that motherfucker rutting into it."

I yanked my hands off her before I wounded her and jumped off the bed. "Isabella, enough. Please."

She sucked in a shuddering breath. "I don't know why I didn't die. Come to think of it, I strongly believe it was Damien's work that night. All of it. Having Declan go psycho on me, and the saving right before I rattled my last breath. The show couldn't just end like that. It wasn't entertaining enough for him. So not only have I ended up losing my baby, almost losing my life, but I had to survive, living with the scars and…a womb that had suffered greatly that miserable night.

"So to answer your question, Joshua, yes, having children matters to me that much." Her dark gaze locked on mine. "My chances to have another child are slim to none. If turning into a beast fixes me up and lets me have a baby even for a short while, I'll take those chances gladly. Any human could die younger than fifty anyway. That doesn't stop them from having kids."

"And so you shall have a child." The wolf's voice penetrated my ears. "With Alec."

My head snapped up toward him. That rabid mutt was out of the picture completely, and now his chances to win Isabella had rocketed to the roof.

I couldn't give her what she wanted unless a fucking miracle happened and I could impregnate her sick womb now, but that only meant she couldn't turn on Halloween or the infant's destiny would be at risk.

Alec could, but he was too jealous to stay.

That left her one option. That smirking wolf over there that had just waltzed in, still playing the Good Samaritan.

"Kayden." She threw herself into his arms. "How long have you been here?"

He took in a deep breath. "Long enough to hear everything."

I was too consumed by my fury to detect

his smell or hear his pulse.

"Where's Alec?" she asked.

His ugly brows hitched. "Don't worry. He will be back."

She fiddled with her thumbnail. "You don't have to lie to me. I know he's left. He doesn't want to be a part of this anymore. Why would he when there's always the next life, right?"

"I know my brother. His stubbornness and temper get in the way sometimes, but he always comes back to his senses."

I rolled my eyes, fed up with the charade. "I'm going out."

Finally, she left the wolf's embrace, and I regained her attention. "You're leaving me, too?"

I savored her beautiful face and stroked her hair. "No, my love. I will fight for you till the last second, even if I know I've already lost. I just need a walk."

"To sink your teeth into something?" Kayden taunted.

"YES! Another moment of listening to your bullshit, and that *something* will be your neck."

"Now who's talking bullshit? In your dreams, bloodsucker." His disgusting voice trailed behind me as I blurred out.

CHAPTER 32

BELLE

The only sun I'd felt on my skin for weeks was through the bay windows. Now, it speckled my face and dress as I strolled down to the clearing I'd only heard of from the boys.

Joshua and Kayden prepared a picnic under the willow tree. Sandwiches, coffee, bourbon. The brown bears were chilling on the other side across from us, rolling in the tangle of grass and wildflowers. It was so beautiful. Peaceful. I even saw a female deer, and out of respect, none of the beasts hunted her.

"Thank you for this. I really needed to go out," I said.

Joshua cradled my hand in his palms and planted a soft kiss on it. "Anything to bring back your beautiful smile."

"You look so beautiful in that red dress. Reminds me of the first day we met in this life." Kayden pecked my cheek.

I chuckled, feeling the rivalry between the two, and blushed at the memory; that red dress of my birthday was barely on me when we met.

My gaze trained on the bears. They looked so cute, playing together, rubbing each other's bellies. "How are they your brothers?"

"Bear father, wolf mother," Kayden answered.

"Is that possible?"

"Yes. We come from an ancient clan of shifters that only breed in twins. Each original parent had chosen their spirit animal and adopted them as their inner beasts. Their children carry the gene. When cross mating happens, which is quite popular in our clan, each twin has the beast of either parent."

"Does that mean if I get pregnant, it will be a wolf twin?"

"*When* you get pregnant, yes." He touched

my belly and smiled. "I can't wait."

A tingling of excitement ran through me as I imagined it. A beautiful twin that looked like Kayden, and him taking care of the three of us, showering us with his kind love.

He cleared his throat. "I mean whether they're mine or Alec's…"

Alec. I hadn't seen him since the night he took off. I sighed and glanced sideways at Joshua, who had his sinister scowl on his face.

Bringing up the baby topic was inconsiderate of me. It wasn't fair to him to be excluded. He'd done everything in his might to protect and love me. And I loved him, too. So much. I wished there had been another way for the four of us to live happily together for the rest of my life.

But all we had was now. The couple of weeks left before Halloween.

"What about you, Joshua? How did you become a vampire?"

He lifted his shadowed gaze to me. "Bitten."

I waited for the rest of the story, but that was all he volunteered. "That's it?"

"Yes." He rose and dusted his pants. "Do you want to go to the creek now before it gets crowded?"

My lips pursed. Seeing him like this tore at

my heart. "Sure. Let's go."

When we arrived, the murmuring waters flowed in my ears, a soothing rhythm of a perfect and permanent stream of waters that deepened the hue of the tree barks. This secluded spot, nestled between acres of greens, instantly took away all the troubles in my head with its beauty. As if land and water came to the most glorious of compromises and made something so spectacularly different from every other place around.

"No one is here. Awesome. We'll have it all to ourselves." Kayden smirked at my dress. "Do you need help taking that off?"

I bit my lip. "I'll only take a dip if all of you come with me. The bears, too."

"As you wish, me lady." He bowed theatrically, and then took off all his clothes, howled a humorous sound and cannonballed naked in the creek.

When he surfaced, he flipped his hair, splashing water all over his face and shoulders. Then he ran his fingers through his hair, looking at me. This wet look made him so much sexier, and even my blood was now clean, that bunny sex drive found me again.

The bears splashed water at him playfully, standing on all fours at the edge of the creek. "Stop it," he yelled at them, his head lashing right and left.

I laughed, my first laugh in weeks, and turned to Joshua. "Are you coming?"

His somber look answered me. "Do you really want me here, Isabella?"

"Yes. Always."

"We do not have always."

"Then I'll take whatever I'm allowed to have with you."

"Remember when we talked about Persuasion? How you hated waiting, and how I loved that time never got in between them? How they waited for each other and in the end they got their happily ever after?"

"Yes."

"Why can't we have this? Aren't you tired of taking only what you're allowed but not what you wanted, what you deserved? I know I am."

His eyes were no longer made of bright steel. They misted with a heartbreaking hint of tears that let mine pour out of my eyes.

"No, please. I can't stand your tears. Forget everything I said, I'm a fool. Don't mind me, please." He embraced the back of my head and pressed me to his chest.

"No, Joshua. You're right. It's not fair. Not to you. Not to me. My idea is selfish and risky. No wonder none of my past lives have done it before. The baby might take away my pain for a while, but I would always end up heartbroken, and so would two of you. Not to mention the child… I have no idea what I'm supposed to do, and with Declan out…"

"It's all right." He held me tighter, rubbing my back gently. "That insect will never harm you again. As for our situation, we still have time to figure it out. There must be something. There has to be. And when we find it, I want you to know I'm ready to accept any arrangement, anything that would give me you."

I nodded, blubbering on his shirt.

"Don't you worry about anything now, please. That's not why we're here today." He slid the sleeves of my dress off my shoulders, and I glanced up at him. His scowl had softened into a small smile. I dared unbuttoning his shirt. God, I'd missed those perfect abs. Then I took care of his pants. His mighty cock swung to the right under his boxers, and I couldn't resist feeling it up.

He hissed. "May I keep my underwear? I don't wish to parade my hard-on in public."

"Not a chance. If I'm losing it, you are, too." I finished pushing down my clothes and stepped out of them, taking my shoes off as well.

He uttered a sound in the back of his throat as he took his time watching my naked body.

"You like what you see, Professor Asher?"

"You know I fucking do." The last piece of clothing shielding him from my hungry eyes dropped to his ankles. "Come here." He kicked his boxers off and carried me caveman-style over his shoulder.

I squeaked as he took us to the water, wolf-whistles and bear huffing growls receiving us.

The water was just the right temperature or maybe I was smoldering with the two muscle hotness surrounding me. Even though the two had seen me naked before, and I fucking came for them, I felt so shy.

But happy.

Kayden glided toward me, yet keeping his distance, not touching me. "You look even more beautiful when you're blushing, Professor."

"I've never…" I looked between Joshua and him and giggled.

"Never gone skinny dipping?" Kayden taunted.

"Never been naked with two men at once, but yeah, that too."

Joshua pushed my hair to the side and kissed my neck. "How do you find it so far?"

My whole body tingled. "So sexy."

Kayden was staring tensely at Joshua. I guessed watching a vampire's mouth near a human's neck would do that to a werewolf.

"How about three men at once not just two?"

My eyes widened when Alec's rough voice filled the air.

Reflexively, Joshua enveloped me with his embrace, letting me feel his need for me poking me in the butt cheek.

"Look who's here," Kayden said as Alec sprinted down the creek and took his jeans and underwear off as fast as his twin had done. These two were not embarrassed by anything. Why would they when they owned such bodies and such cocks?

My third beast dove into the water and surfaced only when he was a couple inches away from me.

I took in his face, my heart dancing on the inside, but I blamed him with my eyes. "You're back. I thought you'd never be back."

"Couldn't stay away from you, sweetheart." His fleshy lips devoured mine, not minding the two men circling us. "I missed you so much. I'm sorry I ever left."

Giddy from that kiss, I licked his taste off me. "You're not mad anymore?"

"No. Sharing is caring."

I snorted a laugh. "You're full of shit."

"I am. The wolves aren't wired to share. Even Dracula here is a possessive motherfucker, but…we're also wired to please our mates, and if sharing is what the mate wants…"

"Stop calling me mate. It's creepy."

"I've always been a creep, and you've always loved it, *mate*."

Kayden splashed him. "Seriously, stop it. It *is* creepy, even for you."

Alec returned the splash. "So have you two done it yet?"

"Quit being a dick." Kayden almost drowned him, grabbing Alec's head down the water.

"Why don't we let these two finish fighting while we do something much more fun?" Joshua was still holding me from behind. He carefully bit my earlobe, sending a jolt of desire down my core.

"Yes," I murmured, and his hand fondled my breast, and then pinched my hardening nipple. I tilted my head back so I could kiss him. His tongue swirled down my throat, extracting a moan or two.

"Hey, this is not how foursomes work." Alec's head jumped out of the water. His voice yanked me out of this pussy-clenching kiss.

"Who said anything about a foursome? I'm not doing that here," I said.

"Why not?" Kayden asked softly.

Joshua's fingers were tracing my sides and the horizontal line right under my belly. It was so hard to focus. "What if someone comes? This place gets many visitors."

"Isn't that what you love the most?" Alec winked. "The bears will be on the lookout. Right, boys?"

One of them gave him the…claw.

I giggled. "I didn't know they could do that." Then Joshua pushed a long finger inside my pussy, and the laughter choked in my throat.

Alec clenched his jaws. "Parasite, could you keep your hands to yourself for a moment until we agree on how this shit is going to work?"

"Well, either of you have a bigger chance to claim Isabella this time. Do you not think I deserve a little more here than the two of you while I still can?" Joshua asked.

"But Kayden hasn't had his chance at all, and you had her when she was a fucking virgin. That changes things."

I smiled at Joshua. "You had me when I

was a virgin?"

"Rena." He shrugged, slipping a second finger inside my pussy.

"Ohhh."

Alec narrowed his eyes at me. "How about your vamp goes for a little sucky sucky, then my brother feeds your beautiful, big pussy what it really needs?"

I slapped a hand on my mouth to stifle the laughter frenzy, Joshua's fingers fluttering inside of me now. I was losing control over my body with arousal and laughter.

"Would you stop this crap? Belle is the one who gets to decide who does what." Kayden peered at me. "Besides, I don't want my first time with you to be like this."

"That settles it then. I get to feel you squeeze around me with your tightness while the twin handles the rest." Joshua set my pussy free, and I mourned the amazing fill, water replacing the heat. "Do you agree, my love?"

I nodded. I really needed him.

And the twin sandwich.

"How are we going to do this here? I need something to lean back or brace myself on. The rocks will be too rough," I said.

"Not for me. I'll rest my back on the rocks and hold you the whole time," Joshua said.

"Okay." I swam with him and the wolves to the most shaded bunch of large rocks. Then Joshua did as he suggested and set me on his lap, my back to his front, his cock fully erected between my thighs, rubbing against my outer lips. He held me by the waist. My breasts were above water level, and anyone could see if they looked close enough.

As it had been since my birthday, the exposure turned me on, and my pussy was soaking with scalding wetness.

Kayden started with small kisses along my neck and shoulders, and then he looked deeply into my eyes before he kissed my lips. It was nothing like our first. No guilt or torture in it. Just passion. Heaps of it.

He grew hungrier, greedier. I reciprocated with equal desire. I wanted it all. Lips, tongue, teeth. Everything.

Jolts of heat sparked through me as Alec's mouth found my nipple, and then Kayden slid down from my lips to my second nipple.

Joshua didn't use his fingers to rub my pussy this time. He held the tip of his cock and teased my clit with it. I moaned loudly, and the three of them took what they were doing up a notch.

I stared at the horizon, chest heaving, hands plunged into the twin's hair. No one was there, and the bears were enough to intimidate any intruders. But what if someone was watching from a distance?

And I didn't mean Damien.

I knew that one was watching, jerking off to the action, and for the love of sin, a fresh gush of arousal burst out of my pussy every time I thought he did.

But what if it was Declan that watched?

I cringed at the thought. This would drive him insane, more than he was. Knowing I was sleeping with someone else, let alone three, could trigger that monster to do something really awful.

Dangerous.

"You're so tense, my love. What happened?" Joshua whispered in my ear.

"I have a feeling Declan is watching us." It wasn't just a feeling. I knew he was. He had to.

He scanned the area with his vampire vision. The twin stopped suckling my nipples and did the same. "There's no one here, Belle."

Joshua confirmed it and kissed my shoulder. "And even if he was, let him. We'll be ready for him whenever he comes."

The kissing, suckling and touching all over my body distracted me for a minute, and my focus shifted to the cock tip penetrating me.

"Are you ready for me, love?" Joshua asked with his hypnotic voice.

I nodded, and he pushed me a little forth. Then he lifted my hips and entered me with one thrust.

My moan echoed to the open sky, and the thrusts of his hips knocked off everything in my head but the sensations he was giving me with his big cock.

A finger was circling my clit now while Joshua fucked me hard and wrapped his hand around my neck, choking me a little.

My breasts bounced, difficult to be contained, even in the big mouths of the wolves. They each cupped one, fondling and squeezing, and alternated on kissing my lips. The finger continued the unbelievable movement over my clit, and Joshua pounded me faster, rougher, his hand tightening around my neck.

A pulse throbbed in my pussy and banged my skull, yet I needed more pressure, more filling.

"Kayden, put your cock in my mouth. Alec, put yours in my hand. I'm almost there, and I want you to come all over me, too."

"Oh, fuck, baby. This is so hot." Kayden rose and lifted one leg up on a rock, holding his huge erection to my face. The pressure on my clit didn't stop, so I guessed it was Alec's finger there. Joshua pushed my back down farther so I could reach. Then Alec shifted on his feet and positioned his hard-on in my fist.

I sucked and stroked and bucked. My pussy clasped around Joshua as he wished, my body welcoming the roughness of his feral fucking and the pressure on my neck. Kayden's huge cock fucked my throat, stretching my mouth and jaws until they hurt. Alec tangled his free hand into my hair, pulling it, while I rubbed him hard and fast.

My eyes closed. I was so dizzy I could pass out. Then my orgasm hit, and I felt as if it was coming out of every muscle of my body, not just my clit.

I wanted to scream, but Kayden's cock was still in my mouth, so I just groaned and groaned until I was filled with hot cum inside my pussy, down my throat, and all over my fist.

Joshua unwrapped his hand from my neck and kissed my back.

Kayden pulled out first. "That was so fucking good. It's okay, baby. You can spit now."

I bit my lip and swallowed instead, glancing at him with mischief.

"Holy fuck. Now I'm hard again," he groaned.

Alec cleaned my hand for me in the water, and then kissed my palm. Then Joshua held my hips and swirled me over his cock that my front was facing him now.

I screamed in fucking awe. His cock was still buried deep inside me, and I didn't fall or slide off. "How did you do that?"

"Did the vamp just do the helicopter?" Alec asked.

"Looks like he did," Kayden answered.

I held on to Joshua's shoulders. "What helicopter?"

"This," he spun me in a full circle over his cock, "is the helicopter."

"Oh my God." I squealed. "Can humans do that?"

"Unsuccessfully. But I can. And I did it because I'm not done with you, and for once I want to make love to you while I'm watching your face." He moved all my hair to the side and leaned in for a kiss, the weight of my hair heavy with all the water. One of the discomforts of having such long hair.

The watching, the hair made me think of one thing.

"What's taking up your mind again?" Frustration tinged Joshua's voice.

"I'm sick of living in fear, especially when I don't have so many years to live. I know I can't prove it, but I'm certain Declan is watching me, enjoying the shitty things he makes me feel in the comfort of his hiding place. So if he isn't making a move on his own, I know what to do to provoke him to come out."

CHAPTER 33

BELLE

FOUR DAYS BEFORE HALLOWEEN

"So? How does it look?" I stared at the boys through the mirror nestled among the black, red and white tiles of the hair salon wall I was facing.

Joshua lifted a shoulder. "You look amazing. As always."

I scowled. "You hate it?"

"No. How do you get that from *you look*

amazing?"

Kayden slapped his arm. "You look perfect, baby. You rock that short hair do."

"Yeah. Can't wait to see how that bounces when I tap that—"

Kayden silenced his brother with another slap on the arm.

The hairdresser cleared her throat, blushing. The three looked at her as if they'd just acknowledged she was in the room. I thanked her, and she removed the waterproof cape off me.

I got off the chair, my hand feeling the bare back of my neck and the volume of my hair layers above it. "I barely recognize myself, but I love it."

"You really look amazing," Joshua said.

"Thank you." I smiled. As much as I'd loved my long hair in the past, it was a symbol of my slavery to Declan and his whims. The power of doing such a simple thing as getting my hair cut had been long taken from me. Now, I had regained it, and it felt so liberating.

I couldn't wait for Declan to see. To go nuts over it. "Time to take a walking tour around Forest Grove."

And so we did for the rest of the day. Then we went back to my place and waited.

Yet nothing happened.

We did the same thing the following day, covering more grounds, making more appearances. The whole town saw me, but Declan didn't.

The feeling that he was watching me never faded, but he was nowhere around.

"He's not here, Belle." Kayden sat next to me on a bench in the park; the last place we visited tonight.

"Maybe the cops were right after all," Alec said. "Let's go home, get you some sleep. There's nothing to worry about anymore."

"Not till we meet the devil on Halloween," Joshua added.

CHAPTER 34

BELLE

I barely got any sleep. Even Joshua's cinnamon tea and snuggling between Kayden and Alec in their wolf form, their soft fur covering me, didn't work. I slipped out of the bed and into the kitchen, desperate for coffee. Joshua was sleeping on the sofa bed, looking…dead.

Vampires had always been hot to me, and when I met one in real life, they got even hotter. But sleep didn't flatter them so much.

I gulped the cold coffee from yesterday straight from the pot. Disgusting in every way, but I didn't care. My mind was a hot mess. I needed to give it something to start working and think straight. Right now.

The idea that Declan wasn't around anymore was impossible to believe. Was I prone to misery or was I too much of a narcissist to believe I was no longer the center of his attention? Whatever the fuck was wrong with me, I couldn't wrap my head around the fact that Declan was gone.

Yet everything logical was telling me so.

I splashed my face with some water, loving the air on the back of neck and shoulders without all the hair. I thought I would need time to get used to it, but I embraced it with no effort.

In my robe, I went down for my mail, looking for any sort of distraction until the boys woke. I opened the mailbox, and a deluge of envelopes and subscription magazines fell onto my chest.

When was the last time any of the boys opened this thing? Seriously, I had three men, and none of them could pick up the fucking mail? I would have done it myself if they hadn't been on my tail even to the fucking bathroom, forbidding me to step outside my own bedroom without a guard, let alone outside the apartment.

I carried whatever I could and shoved the rest back inside. I sifted through the mail. It was mostly scholastic journals, bills and a couple of fashion magazines. I might have been a teacher, but I loved my vanity fix. A thick envelope caught my attention. I opened it on my way up, and I squealed when I saw there was a book inside. Book mail was the best.

Carefully, I got it out, admiring the beautiful cover. Then I opened it, my heart leaping as I anticipated seeing my name signed by one of my favorite authors ever.

My fingers trembled before I fully opened the book as my mind raced to remember one thing. When did I order a signed paperback of this particular book?

I checked the sender address on the envelope, and everything fell off my hands, thudding on the stairs.

Sharp gasps ached in my chest, and I suspected I was about to have another panic attack as I stared at the address of my old house. Declan's house.

Shaking, I bent down and grabbed the book. I knew I shouldn't open it. I shouldn't even touch it. I should just call Detective Magnolia and let her take care of the rest. But I held the cover with quivering fingertips and dared open the book.

Till death do us part.

That was written in red ink under the book title. A heart and a smiley face next to it.

Tears streamed down my face, heavy drops smearing the ink. Still shaking, I looked around me. The feeling that he was watching me now was never stronger.

My blurry gaze fell back on the book, and I noticed a little number in the same red ink at the foot of the page. 126.

It wasn't significant to me or to anything in our fucking relationship, so I figured he must have wanted me to see page 126 in this book. I flipped through the pages until I found the right one. There was a tiny envelope glued to it. I yanked it out and tore it open. A cellphone memory card was inside.

Looking back at the page, I found another number. I almost tore the book as I reached the aimed page. There was another note in red.

The white box.

"What fucking white box?"

I searched the pile around my feet, but I couldn't find anything. I ran back to the mailbox and unlocked it. Rummaging through it, I found a small rectangular box. A cellphone box?

Carefully, I opened it and narrowed my eyes at the little phone nestled there. Already assembled with the memory card slot open. I placed the chip in and turned on the phone.

A video immediately played, and I flinched. It took me a minute to realize it was a video of the hair salon where I'd had my hair cut. There was some muffled sounds of...sobs, and then there was the reflection of a hand stretched on a console in one of the mirrors. My heart thrashed as the camera showed the whole arm and another hand in a black glove holding it by the wrist.

"Is this the hand you used to cut my wife's hair?" Declan's abhorrent voice was calm in the video. But it thundered in my skull.

"No. No no no no no." I quivered, gasping.

The sobs turned into sniveling pleas as a blade shone in the camera light reflection. Then there was a shrieking cry, blood all over the mirror and the console, and a mauled hand separated from the arm.

My jaws opened as widely as possible to let out the scream crushing my ribs, but my voice refused to come out.

The screen went black, and the video ended just like that. I felt like my heart was going to stop. I kept looking around me like a maniac, my jaw hanging low. Suddenly, the screen lit with a second video.

It started with a song. *Look what you made me do* on repeat from this song they kept playing on the radio for months. I loved it, and I loved the singer, but my mind was so fucked up now I couldn't remember the names. The video continued like a presentation. Red text on yellow background slides.

This is what happens to people who take things that are mine.

Better lose the company of three.

Or it will be their dicks you love so much that I will chop next time.

Salty tears ran into my mouth. Then anger rumbled through my bones. "You try, you motherfucker. They will rip your stinky dick before you get to blink."

If you think I can't hurt them, think again.

Yeah, I know what they are.

What? My heart sank to my knees.

Remember the video that got you fired? Your glistening pussy gushing out for your own student?

Oh, that got me so hard right now.

My stomach turned, acid burning my chest

But that's beside the point. I have shot another video that you would absolutely love even more.

The next clip was shot in my apartment. My own bedroom. I didn't need to watch to know what was going to be played. Kayden, Alec and Joshua were there. It was the night the police left and Alec shifted in my bedroom and Joshua bore his fangs at him.

That was all I could take before I went down on my knees, my legs no longer able to carry my weight.

"Isabella," Joshua called out, and he was suddenly standing before me. "What happened?"

I just shook my head at him, tears sticking to my hair and the corners of my mouth.

He wrapped an arm around my shoulder and looked at the screen.

"That piece of shit," he grumbled.

"I told you he was watching. I told you he was watching. I told you he was watching," I repeated hysterically.

"Hey, hey. It's all right. We can track this, and we will find him."

"What if it's a burner? You can't track those," I sobbed.

"We'll figure something out, my love. Just calm down."

The video of the boys finished and another slide appeared.

I hate to be the one that lets the wolf out of the bag.

You will always be mine. So come back to Daddy, Belle.

Alone.

Just call the number on this phone, and I'll tell you where to find me.

Btw, if you call the cops or I get hurt in a mysterious animal attack, this beautiful video and several more of you being the bitch you've always been will be posted online for everyone to see.

Love, Daddy.

Now, I was having that panic attack.

CHAPTER 35

BELLE

"Maybe we should call the cops," Alec suggested hunkered next to me under the willow tree.

"And tell them what exactly?" Kayden stood, blocking the sun, his hands on his hips. "The fucker is blackmailing Belle, and oh look, we're a bunch of shifters and vamps?"

"Do you have anything better?"

"We'll give the phone to someone else to crack it."

"The phone is a high burner. The tech guy

I knew is one of the best, and he couldn't get anything out of it," Joshua said.

The three yammered futile solutions that would never solve anything before they started cursing and kicking stuff.

"I'll go meet him," I mumbled, my head bent over my knees.

"What did you just say?" Alec scoffed.

"You heard me." I lifted my head and glanced at the three of them. "I can't have him hurt anyone else because of me. It's the only way to get him off your backs."

"You will do no such thing. I'd rather get exposed," Kayden said assertively.

"Me too," Joshua agreed, and Alec followed.

"Do you have any idea what you're saying?" I sighed, exhausted. "If anyone knows about what you are, it will turn into a witch hunt. Thousands of painful experiments. Life in a cage. Getting used for doing horrible things. And who knows, maybe they will invent a way to end your lives."

"You know that from your porn books, too?" Kayden joked.

His humor at this moment was too much to conceive. I saw the woman who cut my hair lose her hand and her whole future right before me. I watched a fucking video that would ruin the lives of the men I loved forever. And he was making a fucking joke? I just rose and stomped away.

"Belle, where the hell are you going?" His shout trailed behind me.

"I need a moment alone. Don't follow me."

Footsteps did anyway. I twisted, and it was Joshua at my back. "I said don't follow me."

"Fine. Just tell me where you're going."

"Not meeting Declan if that's what you're worried about."

"I know. I still have the burner that has the number you have to call if you are."

"Then, if you don't mind, and it's not too much trouble, can I, for fuck's sake, have a moment to myself?" I snapped and spun away, not waiting for a response.

"Jeez, someone needs the big D."

"I heard that, Alec!" I shouted as I passed by the grizzly guards.

"I'll get it ready for you just in case, sweetheart. Don't take too long."

I swore under my breath as I stalked into the woods. How could they not understand how much danger they and the entire pack were in?

And it was all because of me.

Because of the psycho I married and

wouldn't let me go. I should just go to him, let him torture me to death and get it all done. It would be the best solution for everyone.

I wished I had been dead the night he tried to kill me. Would I have gone straight to Damien if I had?

My feet stopped short. My glance wandered around the thick trees. Damien…

"If you're here, show yourself. We need to talk."

The wind only carried the sounds of nature. No sign of the devil.

"I know you're here. Just come out. You owe me this much."

I crossed my arms over my chest and waited. But nothing happened. I was just a crazy woman talking to the trees.

I cried against my will, and I couldn't believe I was going to say this, but I did. "Please, Damien. I need your help."

My eyes squeezed shut, and I cringed at my own words, but I had no clue what else to do. I had to do something to save my men. Just like they had once saved me.

"I thought you'd never ask."

I gasped, opening my eyes to see Damien Pattison, standing in front of me, in a blue Armani suit. The devil had style.

"What's the matter? You look like you've

just seen the devil." He chuckled. "That joke never gets old." He took a step toward me, and I jumped back.

"Seriously?" He rolled his eyes. The red tinge in them I'd seen before when he was in my head reappeared. "How can I help you, Professor Ferro?"

My chest rose and fell with every labored breath, and he was staring at my breasts shamelessly. Fuck. "Why did you save me that night?"

"Who said I did?"

"Really? We'll play that game?"

He smirked. "Maybe not."

"Then answer me."

He stepped closer again. This time I let him, and I stared back into his eyes. "I want you to come to me willingly, my queen."

"What?"

"I told you once you didn't know how important you were to me." He circled around me without laying a hand on me, but my skin crawled as if he did. "I've always had my eyes on you. You're the only creature worthy of ruling my kingdom by my side."

I pressed both my thumbnails at the same time. "What the hell are you talking about?"

"Exactly that. Hell. You're my chosen bride, Rena. I want to make you my queen, not just another soul to reap. And for that to happen, you have to take your throne by choice. I couldn't let death ruin it for me. For the both of us." He stopped by my side, his head bent to my ear, his breaths on my neck. "I know you will be mine one day, my queen. You only have a tiny little choice to make, and I've been waiting ever so patiently for you to do just that."

My mind spiraled. "You think I'll willingly choose to go to hell?"

"Hell is not what you think, my queen. It's a kingdom where you can have anything and everything you ever wanted. Where you see the people who have wronged you burn and suffer for all eternity. It's where you have your revenge and end all your fears."

"But—"

"Say all the buts you need, but you know hell is the right kingdom for you, Isabella. It's what you really want. You're just afraid to admit it. But I'm here. I will open your eyes and guide you to your throne. I will never leave you. I will always be by your side. Let me be your king, and I'll serve under your feet. Every wish of yours, I'll make it come true. Your deepest desires I will serve exactly as you want them to be served."

Dizzy, the memory of the orgasm he gave

me attacked me. My body betrayed every thought in my head, and my fucking pussy throbbed. If I just met his tempting face, even though I knew it wasn't fucking real, I would crush my lips into his like the last time.

My desire for him wasn't his doing. He wasn't messing with my head, neither this time nor the last. And that part of me scared the shit out of me.

"Oh," he sighed, amused. "Yes… I love that smell. It assures me you want me as much as I want you." His hand touched my stomach, and it clenched under his fingers. "I can't wait to put my babies in your belly."

You bastard. You're hitting hard on my every need, luring me into your darkness. Why me, Damien? Why me?

His hand left my body. His breath was no longer on my neck, and his feet stepped back.

Only then I dared look at him. "Tell me. Why me?"

"The answer is obvious but too hard to believe."

Was he saying what I thought he was?

"Yes," he answered.

I swallowed, not yet accustomed to acknowledging he was listening to my thoughts. "This can't be."

"I told you it was too hard to believe, but it

is the truth. I'm not sure why you would believe it from a soulless vampire or a vicious predator and not me, though."

"Only because you're the devil," I mocked.

"The devil that is in love with you."

"C'mon, Damien. You're the source of all evil. You have no feelings."

He looked at me as if I'd hurt those nonexistent feelings. "I am not the source of all evil. I just rule its kingdom. If it were up to me, I would eradicate evil and make everyone good and happy. But I don't make the rules."

Suddenly, I was inclined to believe him. And not only that, I wanted to give him a fucking hug. What was wrong with me?

I shook my head and my arms and everything that could be shaken to yank my mind and my body out of his wicked charms. "Can you help me with Declan or not?"

"Depends on how you'd like me to help."

"I want you to find out where he's keeping the videos and erase them completely from everywhere."

"That's it?"

Was it that simple to him? Hope flickered in me. "Yes. Can you do that?"

"At a price."

I wasn't surprised or appalled. In fact, I was prepared and more than ready to pay. "What do you want?"

"You."

I gulped, staring at him for a second. Then I took off my clothes. "Here."

He eyed me with monstrous hunger that hardened my nipples in an instant. "Paying upfront, too? Interesting."

"Let's get it over with."

"And you're doing this selflessly, just for your beasts?"

"Of course." The sane part in me was. The other part was doing it because it really wanted the devil filling me with his cum.

He came closer and stood behind me. His arms snaked around my waist, and his nose dipped into my neck and breathed me in. My breath caught at the sensation, at the thought that I was about to be taken by this beautiful devil.

"As tempting as watching this beautiful body may be, how stupid do you think I am, Isabella?" He swirled me to face him. "You know very well if I have you now, the deal is void, and I'll lose you forever. You really think I'd risk our future for one fuck?"

Fuck, piss and shit. *Way to go, Belle, thinking you can tempt the devil with your fat ass.* "Well, it's the only way you'll have me because I'm never choosing to rule hell with you."

"Never is an exaggerated word, my queen."

"Stop calling me that." I grabbed my clothes off the dirt and put them back on. "I'm ready to do anything to get you to erase those videos, but I won't choose you on Halloween, Damien."

"And I wasn't coercing you to do that. I told you your choice must come willingly for it to work."

"Then what do you want me to do?"

"That Halloween night, I want to be there."

"I'm confused. Aren't you going to be there already?"

"When you choose your beast, you will mate before the willow tree to seal the deal. I want to be there, in the flesh, not only in your head. I want you to see me come for you while you're coming for another, and I want you to look me in the eye when he is making you orgasm."

My panties were melting. They must have been because my juices had reached my inner thighs. "Why would you do that? You've already watched me come a million times. I know you've been watching every naked and sexual moment of mine all my lives. Plural."

"But you've never watched me. Something tells me you'll enjoy your claim more, come even faster when you see the devil *jizz* to your beautiful screams of pleasure. And perhaps, it will grow your appetite enough to crave the devil's cock for dessert."

"Not in this lifetime," I lied. I wanted that very much.

"I'll take my chances. And if it doesn't happen in this lifetime, there's always the next. Patience is my game, Isabella." He smirked.

"Fine. I'll do what you want. I'll watch you while you watch me, but that's it."

"Do that, and I'll erase the videos. You and your beasts will have nothing to worry about ever again. Not even me."

"Only till my next self is reborn."

He nodded once.

I took a deep breath. "I'll take it."

He stuck a hand out. "Shake on it?"

My heart thudded as I stretched a quivering hand. Then I looked the devil in the red eyes and shook his hand.

CHAPTER 36
BELLE

"You did what?" Alec yelled at me. It was the first time he or any of the boys had yelled at me.

All four of us were at Joshua's loft, where we technically lived now that we had no doubt my apartment was bugged. The twin had offered to let me stay at their lodge in the woods, but that territory was dominated by shifters, and Joshua wasn't very welcomed there.

Joshua clasped his hands together, his fingers intertwined, as he leaned forward, sitting by the fireplace. "How could you make a deal with the devil, Isabella? Haven't you learned anything?"

I bent my legs under me. My gaze drifted from the brick walls to the sun setting behind the floor to ceiling windows. "Your deal with Damien saved my ass. Mine will save yours."

"Damien? Oh, you're on a first-name basis now? With the fucking devil?" Alec paced from one couch to another, his shouting giving me a headache.

"What was I supposed to do, Alec?"

"Not that! Nothing at all. Did any of us ask for your help?"

I pinched the bridge of my nose. "I saw an opportunity, and I took it. I don't know why you're making it a big deal. He didn't ask for much. It's just…voyeurism."

"HE IS SEDUCING YOU!" He threw his hands in the air, and then turned to his brother. "I can't. Just… Talk to her. Put some sense in her head. Make her see what this truly is." He twisted at me. "Can't you see what this is? How can you not see what this is?"

"Stop yelling at me."

He swore, running both his hands through his thick hair, and threw himself on a chair.

I glanced at Kayden, waiting for him to lash out, too, but he was silent. His eyes said everything he needed to say. The blame, the rage…the fear.

I lifted my chin to stop myself from crying. "Stop looking at me like that. You have something to say, just say it."

His jaws tightened, and then he let out a deep, heated breath. "You want to have sex with Damien, don't you, Belle?"

Stunned at the bluntness, I just shifted my stare from one angry face to another. I didn't want to answer that question. Not out in the open like that. I was struggling with the truth myself, having a hard time accepting it.

"Well, he knows that. He wouldn't have dared go into your head and touch you if you hadn't let him in." Kayden faced me like a brutal mirror.

"Even so, the main reason I accepted his deal was to save you," I mumbled.

"But Damien does want to seduce you. He knows one man is not enough for you, and you'll be sad having to choose one. He also knows that at a claim, your sex drive will be at its highest. You will want to have more, and he will be there, making that connection he's already made with you. There is a big chance, with the sadness and the heightened desire, you will let him have you at that moment."

I blinked. Many times. "Let's assume I did

that, what's the worst that can happen? I would have already chosen. He can't have my soul. I'll still belong to my mate."

"Oh for crying out loud!" Alec kicked something. I was too distracted to see what it was. He jumped to his feet and paced the room again. "Let's pretend your mate will be okay with sharing you with the fucking devil on claim night. But what if you're not? What if you decide to switch sides?"

Anger surged in me. "Why would I do that?"

"Who the fuck knows? Why would you want to screw the devil in the first place? Who knows what happens, what changes in you when he's actually inside of you?"

The questions hit me like heavy slaps on the face. None of them crossed my mind when I'd made that deal. I was truly blind to the consequences, thinking I had outsmarted the devil when he was the one who played me. How could I not see any of that logic?

"You're right." My head spun. "He made it look like I was in control, actually winning, while he knew all along that's exactly what would happen on Halloween night." I clutched my stomach, where Damien had touched me. "What was I thinking? With my mentality, with that side that craves him and scares the hell out of me? He blinded me. He…did what the devil always does, and I listened."

"Yes, my love," Joshua said, his somber expression never leaving him.

"And sadly, we have no jurisdiction in hell. We can't save you there." Alec wasn't being sarcastic now. I could hear his pain behind the ugly truth.

"All what we can hold on to now is our faith in you, Belle. Our faith in your good side. The question is, do you have that faith in yourself?" Kayden became my mirror again, yet this time, my reflection was a complete blur.

CHAPTER 37
KAYDEN

HALLOWEEN NIGHT

It was cold even for the end of October, as if all the heat had been drained away into the earth. Through the road rose the werewolves, the devils, the vampires and the monsters. The fake ones not the real. The real beasts wore tuxes, and their waiting bride was in a white dress with flowers in her hair.

The bride I'd never had.

She was with me in the truck as I drove to the woods. Alec had gone with the vampire to the clearing. The bears didn't want to be there as always.

"You look so handsome in that tux," she said.

I tried to smile. "Thank you. You look…so beautiful. Your mate, whoever he is, is a very lucky bastard."

"Thanks. I guess." He inhaled deeply and let that breath out slowly. "Kayden…"

"Yes, baby?"

"Why haven't you… Why are you still waiting? Tonight is the night all this ends, and there's a good chance it won't end well. Why haven't we had our time together? Do you not want me?"

"Of course, I want you. There has been no time when I didn't want you."

"Then why?"

I pulled over at the end of the trail and held her amazing gaze. "Because I'm hoping that will give you something to make you want to hold on to this life. Unfinished business of sorts."

She laughed, but then she burst into tears.

I was barely holding myself together. Watching her cry would shatter me in pieces. "Baby, please don't cry. You're going to…ruin your makeup."

She threw herself onto my chest. "It doesn't matter. It's not like it's a real wedding."

I lifted my silent scream to the moon as I embraced her like I would never see her again. "C'mon, baby. It's going to be okay. I love you, and I have faith in you. I know you'll do the right thing."

She drew back. "The right thing? What would that be, Kayden? What the fuck would that be?"

I drowned in the hazel eyes. "Whatever makes you the happiest."

Her lips met mine in a heated kiss that lasted forever and ended too soon. When she pulled away, her lips were swollen, and I was burning. Another minute, and I wouldn't be able to hold back anymore.

I pushed the door open and jumped out. Then I helped her outside, and carried her to the clearing so that her dress wouldn't get dirty.

Under the willow tree, the four of us stood. No spoken words, only emotions thudding in our chests, and miserable thoughts spiraling in our heads.

The air felt sticky despite the chill, and I knew he had arrived. The devil manifested in the dark with his deep eyes and deceiving face.

My blood simmered. The beast clawed at me, itching to rip apart the fucker who came to steal the love of my life away.

"You look dashing, gentlemen," Damien said and bent to kiss Belle's hand. "And you, you look like a queen tonight."

"Stay away from her." Alec was about to lunge at him, but Asher and I held his arms.

"Always the reckless Beastly. I love that quality about you. Makes my work so easy."

"Fuck you."

"Enough." Belle shouted. "Damien, don't be a dick. Not tonight."

He smirked. "As you wish, my queen."

She rolled her eyes. "Do you have the videos?"

He reached into the inside pocket of his tux jacket and brought out a CD, a couple of flash drives and a few chips. "Here are the copies. I also deleted the originals from the hard drives."

"Are these the only ones, Damien?"

"You really think I need to make *digital* copies for myself?"

"Of course not. You have them all stored in your disgusting…" She snatched them from him and gave them to Asher. "Can you check?"

He let go of my brother's arm, took the chips and worked them one by one in his phone. He muted the sound and skimmed through the videos. After all, there were *sensitive* clips of Belle in there, too. Then he nodded. "It's all here."

She sighed in relief. "So how does this work?"

"We wait for the witch to do the ritual," I said. "She will ask you for your choice. Then you claim your mate and finish the turn according to the clan you've chosen."

"Witch? What witch?"

"The one who helped us make the deal."

"And the witch has arrived."

Belle gasped, twisting at the voice. "No fucking way."

CHAPTER 38

BELLE

"Katrina!"

She held the tail of her green dress to the side and tilted her hip, her other hand carrying a tote. "Surprise."

"Surprise? How? What? You're a fucking witch?" *Bitch*.

She barely kept her balance in those nine-inch heels as she walked on the grass to the willow tree. "Not just *a* witch, sweetie. The one who helped those dickheads save your life."

My eyes widened, and my jaw fell. I didn't care if I looked like a lemur or a lame ass hyena. "You were a teenager when I met you."

"Yeah, that was a spell that made me look like a teen. You know, magic is what witches do." She reached me and gave me a fucking hug. "How are you holding up, sweetie?"

I pushed her off me. "I... You're unbelievable. All this time you've been lying to me, and my mom."

"Oh no. Your mom was a witch too, from our coven. I sent her to take care of you after your parents passed away. It was very sad that she died."

The French Quarter in New Orleans. Of course. "You know what happened to my parents?"

"Cursed bloodline. They died in an unfortunate accident, and now are guests in Damien's...realm."

My head was going to explode. I revolved in circles, peering at the darkness and the creatures that turned my life upside down. "I need a fucking minute."

"Take your time, sweetie. We have all night," she said.

My whole life was a lie. Everything was never mine. I had no control. No choices whatsoever. Every minute was designed to bring me to this one. Every person was fit in it to deliver me here.

To Damien.

The devil that played us. Broke us all.

To have his queen.

And it only took two hundred and fifty years. In his time, it was nothing.

Well played, Damien. Well played.

I breathed in the air, savored its taste, felt the coolness fill my lungs. I touched the grass and the tree, smelled the flowers, watched the moon. I stared at the people I loved, memorized their features, their scents, the rhythm of their heartbeats.

I kissed each one of them and licked the taste. I laughed and then cried. And I felt the love in my heart, said my goodbyes and felt the ache, carved it all in my mind before my soul. As I might never feel any of that the same way ever again.

My breath shuddered on my lips. "I'm ready."

The boys and I held hands in a circle while Katrina got sage and strange stones out of her tote. She placed them in a specific order, said some voodoo words and lit the sage.

My soul was being ripped out of me, torn into a million pieces and then sewed together with the souls of my past lives. I'd become

Rena and all her reincarnations all at once, and I saw their lives, the happiness and the sufferings.

And the choices they had made.

Katrina peered at me. "Have you made your choice?"

This was it. The one moment I truly got to choose.

The decision that would either start a happy life for me or end mine and Rena's forever.

Joshua, Alec and Kayden beseeched me with their glistening eyes under the moonlight. Damien's red stare blazed at me, a genuine smile on his face, one you saw on the faces of grooms while Here Comes the Bride played at their weddings.

He was happy.

The potential of me choosing him wasn't an evil demonic quest. It was his happily ever after.

"Isabella, have you made your choice?" Katrina repeated, and everyone was looking at me.

It was all clear in my head now. I did have a choice. "Yes," I said, confidence brewing inside me.

"Who do you choose to be your mate this lifetime?"

"Kayden."

Kayden squeezed my hand. Sighs and swears filled the air. Joshua's gaze dropped to the ground. Alec kicked at the dirt.

"And Joshua…" I added, and his head snapped up. "And Alec." He stopped kicking and glanced at me, his expression a question mark.

"You can't do that," Damien thundered. "You have to choose one."

"No. The deal stated I had to make a choice. It didn't say anything about choosing just one mate." I stepped out of the circle and reached Damien. "It's the twenty-first century. Ever heard of polyamory? A woman can choose to have multiple partners at the same time, have a big, happy family together."

His eyes flamed. I was positive if I touched him now, I would burn myself.

"What's hurting you the most now? That you lost me this lifetime? Or that I outsmarted you for once?" I asked.

A dull shadow crossed his face. "Hope."

"Hope?"

"What hurts me the most is that this time I actually had high hopes you would finally be mine. I even refurnished the home I'd prepared for us, had a huge ceremony awaiting your arrival."

"You were counting on our deal to get me as horny as possible so I'd mate with you, too, and choose you instead?"

"Yes," he confessed. "But now you have three mates. I don't think you'll need me anymore."

I twisted my lips. "You give up that easily?"

He gave me a quizzical look. "What are you telling me, Professor?"

"There's always a part of me that will want you, Damien. If I suppress it or ignore it, it will come back to bite me later, and it won't be pleasant. I'm telling you if the part when you said you were in love with me is true, you will fight for me, make sacrifices—"

"I'm ready to unleash hell on earth to have you, Isabella. If you will take me."

"Here's a new deal for you. I wouldn't be your hell queen. Not a big fan of fire. But I'll let you be a part of my kingdom here on earth?"

"Share you? With the beasts?

I nodded. "No more reincarnations. No more pain. We all live forever. A Happily ever after for all."

He glared at me for long, nerve-wrecking moments.

"I'm sure you're smart enough to know it's a great deal." I tried not to give him too much time to think. "The only deal where you get to have me. In the flesh you love so much."

"I do. But believe it or not, I love your heart even more. Do I have that, too?"

"My sweet devil, you know I've already saved you a spot."

His notorious smirk curved up his mouth. "Your deal is very tempting."

I stretched my hand out. "Shake on it?"

"Professor Ferro, you never cease to amaze me." The smirk grew into that full genuine smile. Then he squeezed my hand in a firm shake.

I looked the devil in the red eyes. "And Damien."

CHAPTER 39

BELLE

Katrina looked at me like I was a nutcase, waving burning sage at me. "Isabella, you have chosen four mates on this Halloween night. Is that your final decision?"

"Yes." I smiled.

Her shoulders slumped. "And you? The four of you agree to be Isabella's eternal mates on earth?"

The four mumbled their yeses, and I chuckled.

"Seriously, how is this going to work? The

first step of this union is to fuck. The five of you will fuck at the same time?"

I shrugged. "Yeah. It's fun. You should try it at least once in a lifetime."

She burst into laughter. "Assuming this kinky shit works, what about the biting? You think your body can take double wolf, vampire and devil bites?"

"It's the only way to get their venoms to mix into my blood so I can turn into…"

"Into what, sweetie? They don't have a name for you yet."

A werewolf and a vampire mix was a hybrid. But what would a third vampire, third shifter, third devil be?

"We should just call it Belle," Alec suggested.

"I like the sound of that. So when I have my babies, will they be…Belles?" My excitement never seemed to touch Katrina.

"They will have your blood, yes," she said.

"We're a having a Belle twin." Kayden rolled it in his mouth. "I love that."

Katrina waved a dismissive, sage holding hand, mumbled more voodoo words and gestured at the willow tree. "You may now have your gangbang."

A giggle burst out of me. "This is not a gangbang—"

"Yeah, yeah, enjoy your harem, sweetie. I'll go grab me some booze until you're done. It's going to be a long night."

My harem. I'd always thought these things only happened in books—porn books. Now, I did have my own harem, and they were smoking hot.

"Who are you going to start with, Professor?" Joshua smiled.

I looked for the golden strikes, and they were sparking for me. "Kayden."

"Of course," Joshua said. "We'll take a hike while you enjoy your first time. Holler when you're done. We're a blur away."

"I'm not leaving. I have to be here for my twin on his big night." Alec punched Kayden in the arm.

Kayden returned the punch. "Fuck you very much. I don't need you here."

They were about to have another one of their annoyingly cute fights, but I was too excited, too horny to wait it out. "Alec, go!"

"Oh, man. Why did he get to walk in on us, and I don't get to stay?"

"We were done when he did, and you will get to walk in on us when we finish. You'll get to do a lot more than that."

He grunted, and he seemed to be picturing it in his head. "Yeah."

I laughed and shooed him with my hand. "And Damien, no peeking."

The devil bowed at me as he walked away with my vampire across the clearing. Alec ran to catch them, and Kayden and I were alone at last.

He twined his fingers into mine. "I love you."

"I love you, too."

"Would you like me to tear your dress off or would you like to take it off yourself?"

I bit my lip, watching the glowing strikes. "I thought you'd never ask. Tear it off, please"

One yank and I was naked in front of him. Quickly, he got rid of his tux, his huge body magnificent under the moonlight. He made a bed under the tree with his clothes, carried me and laid me down on it.

He kissed me ever so softly, as if I was going to break. His fingertips brushed against my skin, taking their time, studying my curves, tracing my scars.

"Will these be gone when I turn?" I whispered.

His palm spread my thighs. "Yes. Not that they're taking anything away from your beauty." His lips trailed down them with little, wet kisses. Then he licked me where he parted my legs, the sensitive areas on my inner thighs, and I trembled.

He took one look into my eyes, and then he took in my pussy. I loved that look, that gaze before he did anything with it. The golden strikes blazed, and he went all in, nose, lips, tongue, unleashing a beautiful fire in my core.

"Kayden, I want to touch you."

He slurped my juices, yet kept me wet with his big tongue. "Touch me all you want, baby. I'm yours."

"Come here then. You're so big."

He shifted his weight on his elbows and lay on top of me, keeping a fair distance so he wouldn't crush me. I felt his hard skin and incredible muscles in his arms, chest and abdomen. So strong, so beautiful and hot. My hands slid up and down his thighs and then squeezed that rock hard ass. His cock grew longer with every touch that it was now pressing on the top of my pussy.

I moaned. "Are you going to bite me while we're…"

"Yes." He said between kisses on my neck. "That's how it works."

I was a little afraid. A lot more wet than afraid, though. "Okay. I guess I'm ready."

"Good. I can't bear another second of

waiting." He spread me farther, as far as possible, and pushed just the tip inside me. I gasped as it slid easier than I anticipated. The second thrust stretched me well, and his groan set a throb in my pussy.

My gasps and his groans mingled as I managed to take all of him. "Fuck, you really have a big pussy, and it's so fucking tight. How is that possible?"

His cock was pushing up to my stomach. It was hard to speak or even think now. "Who cares? Less words. More thrusts."

"Yes, baby." He prowled up over my quivering body, his lips and tongue and hands worshipping more of my skin. His swollen length pushed into me again, claiming my body as his lips claimed mine. He kissed me as if my kiss was the only one he'd ever need. As if my lips were the only lips he'd ever want. His thick erection moved within me in long, unhurried strokes as if I was the only mate he'd ever fuck.

I locked my ankles behind his back, our open mouths slanting together again and again, addicted to the possessive thrust of his tongue, to the breathtaking intensity of his kiss. My fingers buried in his hair. I rocked with him, loving every sultry taste past his lips, every endless slide of his cock.

He slammed into me, growling into my mouth. My eyes rolled back as I clenched around him. When I opened them, he wasn't kissing me anymore. His jaws were bigger, and canine fangs elongated out of his mouth.

"Oh my God." My fear and arousal surged at once. He turned his head and bit into my neck—hard, so fucking hard, but nothing ever hurt so well. Ecstasy jolted through my veins like lightning, electrifying every muscle in an erotic, savage shock that jagged straight to my pussy. My hips punched upward, orgasm erupting in violent spasms.

Holy fuck. *Holy fuck.*

Heart pounding, I stared back at his eyes, now glowing in full, not just strikes. His mouth was covered in my blood, and he was howling, his cock filling me with his cum.

His face returned back to normal, and he kissed around my wounded neck tenderly. "Are you okay?"

"Yes, but it was so intense."

"I know, baby. It was so fucking hot. Now, you're really mine. Once you'll turn, you'll need to bite me, too, and I'll be all yours."

My head spun with all the new mechanism of things. "Am I bleeding?"

"No." He smiled.

"Good." My pussy was still throbbing, and

his cock never eased out. I looked down "Is this a knot?"

He looked down as if he'd forgotten he was inside me. "No. This is just what you're doing me. Your pussy is making me so fucking hard even if I'd just had the strongest spurts of my life. You'll know the knot when it really happens."

"Okay." I gasped a laugh. "One down."

He tilted his head back, not sharing my humor. Then he pulled out of me as slowly as possible. I moaned at the unbearable emptiness he'd left in me. I needed to be filled again. Fast.

When he moved off me, I saw the other three coming back. They were standing in front of me in a flash. Silver, golden and red eyes ogling my naked body. Beasts all looking like they wanted to devour me.

"We heard the howl," Alec said, glancing at his brother's hard cock. "Nice job, Bro."

My abdomen clenched with a laugh, and I was pretty sure the moisture spilling out of my pussy was Kayden's cum.

Alec trailed it with his stare. "Eager to have those Belles, huh?"

Kayden chuckled, and I was dying with embarrassment. I shut my legs. "Could you all get naked now? This is getting really awkward."

"Sure, love." Joshua started, and the other two stripped.

I sat up, rising on my elbows, sore from the bite, three dicks flying my way. I could get pregnant just by looking at how big they were. With the cum already swimming in my pussy and with more to follow, the chances to conceive my Belles tonight were magnificent.

Curious, I raked Damien's body from head to cock. It was the first time I saw him naked. He was sculpted into my version of perfection. I knew it was just a camouflage, a delusion to get me melting like that, but I couldn't care less. And his cock...didn't disappoint in either length or girth.

Boy, it is going to be a long, wet night.

I bit my lip. "Professor Asher, would you do the helicopter with me while the devil watches?"

It was one of the rare times that I heard Joshua laugh. "Gladly." He scooped me up, perched down and settled me on his lap—his hard cock. "Watch and learn, Devil."

"I will." Damien winked at me.

Joshua and I were sitting so that my back was to the tree and his to Damien. Alec sat next to his brother, rocking his leg impatiently.

My vampire grabbed my waist and pushed me down on him while his hips moved up. My breasts bounced in his face, my moans loud, my arms clasped behind his neck.

He nuzzled my neck. "I love your smell."

Was it too weird that I got wetter knowing it wasn't my smell he loved, it was the smell of my blood? I took a look at his face, and his eyes were already dark and dilated, his fangs peeking under his lip. I never wanted to be bitten by a vampire more than now.

His teeth grazed my skin as he pounded into me. My gaze wandered between his and Damien's. The devil was licking his lips, eyeing me being taken by another beast. I looked down, and he was fucking his fist already.

I bucked into Joshua, my eyes pinned to the devil's cock. Joshua spread his legs and swung me around in a full circle. Then he fucked me some more and did it again. How slippery Kayden's cum had made my pussy, and how wet Joshua was making me as he fucked me helped a lot with the helicopter. The friction of that move drove me insanely wild. His cock was reaching every nerve ending, every fold.

"Damien, I'm close. Can you come on my chest when I do?" I demanded between moans.

He growled a sound that originated somewhere deep and scary. And so fucking hot.

Joshua screwed me faster. "Careful not to get any on my face. I have wolf cum on my junk. Don't need Satan's milk on my face, too."

Then I felt it. The prick of sharp fangs on my throat, and the ripple of my orgasm in my core.

Joshua bit and sucked and came at the same time. My soul was being drawn slowly out of me. My blood slowed down, too. My orgasm made me hot and unaware of the pain, yet the bite made my limbs cold.

"It's all right. You're going to be all right." Damien got closer and took my lips into his with enough heat to wake the dead. He moaned into my mouth, and hot liquid spurted on my chest.

I kissed him hard, pushing my hips down on Joshua, squeezing the vampire to the last drop, extending my orgasm as far as I could. He was off my neck now, licking my blood on his teeth and what was left on my neck. His venom along with Kayden's must have collided already because I was feeling much better, virile with the bunny sex drive at its highest.

Tangled in need, I wanted more. So much more. Greedy, I knew. I'd just come twice, but it wasn't enough.

Joshua lifted me gently and rested my back to the tree trunk. "When you're done, come drink my blood for the transition to be completed."

"Then I'll have to bite you, too?" I asked.

"Yes." He kissed me softly and made room for Damien.

I welcomed the devil's weight on my rejuvenated body. Some of his cum was spilling along the sides of his cock, and it looked so sexy. I wanted to lick it off. I wanted to taste Satan's milk.

He crawled until his cock reached my lips, and gave me a devilicious smile. Of course, he was in my head.

I made a fist around his shaft and licked the tip. I couldn't believe I was holding the devil's hard cock in my hand, licking his cum. I sucked it, all of it. He tilted his head back, groaning, his hands squeezing my breasts that were already covered in his seed.

Freeing his erection from my mouth, I dug my nails in his firm ass. "I need you inside me now."

"C'mon! I can't believe you're leaving me

for last," Alec grumbled.

"You were her first. It's only fair," Damien said, moving back. He lifted my legs and rested my ankles on his shoulders. Then he pushed all of his cock inside me at once.

I moaned hard.

"Finally," he growled, his thrusts teasing my pulsing clit. He took me hard, touched and tasted me with hunger I'd never seen or felt before. He didn't leave a spot on my body that he didn't either kiss or touch. And when he was done with my front, he flipped me on my stomach and explored my back with equal thoroughness.

"You have a virgin ass, but I won't claim that now. I'll just tease it with my finger while I fill that pussy," Damien said.

I lifted my ass more for him without thinking. "Yes, please."

Fucking me faster, he spat on my asshole, then dipped his pinkie in my pussy and used the wetness when he pushed it into my ass.

"Scream for me. I've always loved to hear your screams of pleasure for others. Now, I want to hear them knowing they're all for me."

My fingers dug in the dirt as he hammered my pussy with his wonderful, perfect, engorged cock, and his little finger fucking into my ass. I screamed. Fuck, I screamed so hard for the devil himself.

"Are you going to bite me, too?" I screamed again.

"No. I'll cut you with my horn." He swiveled me, and my eyes widened at the sight. He had full grown thick horns on his blond head, coiling at the ends with sharp tips.

He stopped moving for a second. "Too scary for you?"

I just stared for a while. "When you're done carving me, I want to hold on to them as you come inside of me."

A mischievous laugh ripped out of his throat. "That's my girl."

He carved my chest with his horn while he slammed into me, the pain suddenly so beautiful. Then I held on to the horns and watched as his eyes turned into a red hell pit, and his hot jizz sent another shivering orgasm down my spine.

I had Alec after Damien. And after the last wolf claimed me, and I carried all four seeds inside me, I drank Joshua's blood.

"Damien, do I need to do anything to finish turning into one third devil?" I asked.

"No. And you won't see my mark on your flesh either. It's already healed. But it's carved on your soul. Once you have your horns, you can mark me, too. Not that you need it to claim me. You know I'm all yours."

I looked down at the fading mark, and old scars that looked like they had never existed, and smiled.

"Shit. We forgot something," Alec said.

I frowned. "What is it?"

"Because you were not born but bitten, and you have vampire's blood in your system, you won't complete your transition as a shifter unless…"

"Unless I kill someone," I finished the sentence for him.

"Yes."

I looked at the night sky with its bright moon and stars, seeing it as if for the first time, dangerous yet delicious temptations swirling in me. "No worries. Joshua, make the call."

CHAPTER 40

Belle

I went into my apartment alone, Declan's phone in my hand, my heart and stomach cold as ice. My feet felt their way in the dark as I closed the door. I turned on the lights and swallowed. "Declan?"

Nothing answered me. I pressed my nail as I walked to the living room. "You said to meet you here. It's very smart of you. No one will ever think to look for you in my apartment."

Silence remained my only companion.

"I haven't told anyone where I am. No one

is following like you asked." I turned on my heels, looking at the empty room. "I can assure you I'm alone. You're making me nervous. Please, come out."

I checked the bedroom, kitchen and bathroom but the place was empty. The phone boomed in my hand. I jumped with a shivering gasp. Then I answered. "I'm here as you asked. Where are you?"

"I had to make sure no one was following you," Declan said.

"No one knows where I am. No one is coming."

"For your friends' sake, I hope it's true. I left you a little gift in your wardrobe. Wear it until I come up." The son of a bitch hung up.

I shoved the phone into the pocket of my jacket and went into my bedroom. Opening the wardrobe, I found a sheer babydoll glaring at me.

Bile filled my stomach and I slammed the wardrobe shut, almost breaking it.

A key turned into my door, and my heart leapt. I froze in place, listening to the footsteps until I saw him coming through the room.

Declan's sickening gaze behind professor glasses hovered over my body. The smile of a psychopath stretched on his face as he moved closer. "My sweet, Belle. We meet again."

My mouth too dry to swallow, I nodded. "That's close enough."

"You're telling me you didn't miss me at all?" He reached a hand to my face, and I slapped it away.

His disgusting smile widened. Then his fist was in my hair and the back of his other hand ringing on my jaw, throwing me on the floor. Before I could recover, he grabbed me up and pushed me on the bed. "Didn't I tell you to wear my gift?"

"I'm not wearing that thing for you," I said between my teeth.

"You prefer to spread your legs naked for three men at once but not wear dirty lingerie for your husband?"

"You're not my husband."

He cackled, his hand reaching in his back. Then the laughter stopped, and a gun was in my face. "Say that again, and you'll have a lovely bullet in your pretty head."

My hands lifted in surrender as my heart pounded violently against my ribs. "What do you want, Declan?"

"You. I wish I could get a fucking whore like you out of my head, but I just can't. I'm obsessed with that face, that body, that filthy cunt you let other men defile. You're mine,

Belle. It's either I have you or no one else does." He waved the gun at me. "Strip."

A strange calmness washed over me. "No."

He unlocked the gun safety.

"You don't say no to me! I said fucking strip, you bitch."

"Or what?"

"I will shoot you, and then I will fuck your dying body just like the last time."

I nodded. "Okay. Why don't you try?"

"Oh, you're not scared of death anymore?"

"Not at all. And I'm done being scared of you, too. So shoot me, Declan. Take your best shot."

His face turned crimson as he swooped down on me, pinning my wrists to the bed. I fought with my new strength, shoving him off me in a flash. I ran outside, but his heavy hands were on my jacket, and he hurled me against a wall. I tried to stand, but a loud bang echoed in my skull.

Fuck. The son of a bitch did shoot me.

In the head.

I crumbled down on the living room floor, blood streaming down my forehead, nose and eyelids.

"Yeah, you stay down while I fuck you nice and hard. I know you missed Daddy's cock." He set the gun on the coffee table and unbuckled his belt.

I was not being dragged into the darkness like the last time. I was aware of everything. My body was eating me up from the inside out, burning with beasts' healing powers.

Wow.

My brain was repairing itself. My skull bones were coming back together. I opened my eyes, laughing softly.

"What the fuck?" Declan's hands froze on his pants.

"I know, right?" I leaned on my elbows and stood.

"W…what… I… You…" he stammered, stumbling back on the furniture. "If you do anything stupid, the videos will be online the next minute."

"Your videos are long gone. And so will you and your nasty shit forever." I closed the distance between us and grabbed his neck.

"Belle, no," he rattled.

I giggled. "I came here craving revenge, pain and blood. I was going to torture you, take my time before I gave your soul to Damien, but…you're not even worth it. I'd rather spend that time fucking my beasts like a whore from hell."

His eyes bulged like a choking fish. "You can't kill me. You can't kill me!"

"Yes, I can. And I will. Goodbye, Professor Montgomery. Fuck you very much." My fingers pressed his throat with all my strength until it snapped. Then I heard it, the beast that rumbled in my core.

The shifter transition was now complete. When my fingers retracted into claws, there was no doubt about it.

"Look at that. I got my claws." With them, I slashed Declan's neck and separated his head from his body.

I lifted my head to the ceiling, sweltering with three different kinds of dark power. Finally, I was free from my captor. Liberated of everything that had ever held me down. I had to become a mixture of three creatures of night and a murderer for it to happen. But this incredible feeling, this dangerous yet exhilarating power was worth it.

With my dark side, I knew I would need a lot of work and time to tame the new power, but I wasn't worried. I had all the time in the world, and four marvelous beasts to help.

Licking Declan's disgusting blood off my hands on my way out of the building, I saw my four beasts standing, waiting for me in the woods.

They were all smiling at me with pride and love.

I was happy at last. No more fear. No more pain. No more monsters.

Only Belle.

And her loving beasts.

THE END

Thanks for Reading!

What a ride ☺ I hope you enjoyed reading All the Teacher's Pet Beasts as much as I loved writing it.

Write a review on amazon or Goodreads

Sign up for my Newsletter on njadelbooks.com

The rest of the series continues with three more installments that complete this universe. Read the now complete series

Remember, Do NOT do the helicopter!

Also by N.J. Adel

Paranormal Reverse Harem
All the Teacher's Prisoners
All the Teacher's Little Belles
All the Teacher's Bad Boys

Reverse Harem Erotic Romance
Her Royal Harem: Complete Box Set

Contemporary Romance
The Italian Heartthrob
The Italian Marriage
The Italian Obsession

Dark MC and Mafia Romance
I Hate You then I Love You Collection
Darkness Between Us
Nine Minutes Later
Nine Minutes Xtra
Nine Minutes Forever

Acknowledgments

Hannah, thank you for reading with me, catching those typos and all the amazing things you do for me.

Shannon, Yashira, Gina, Kasha, thank you so much for your support, spreading the word about my books everywhere.

Sam, Ariel, I love you for needing to read my books before anyone else.

My readers, as always, I FLOVE YOU.

ABOUT THE AUTHOR

N. J. Adel, the author of All the Teacher's Pets, Her Royal Harem, The Italians, and I Hate You then I Love You series, is a cross genre author. From chocolate to books and book boyfriends, she likes it DARK and SPICY.

Mafia bosses, psycho anti-heroes, bikers, rock stars, dirty Hollywood heartthrobs, supes, smexy guards and men who serve. She loves it all.

She is a loather of cats and thinks they are Satan's pets. She used to teach English by day and write fun smut by night with her German Shepherd, Leo. Now, she only writes the fun smut.

Printed in Great Britain
by Amazon